Mark Bickerton has many writing and producing credits in TV, radio and theatre. He is known principally for his work on soap operas such as *Coronation Street* and *Emmerdale* but is now working with his first love of prose. *Day Return to Cocoa Yard* is his debut book. As a storyteller and writing consultant, Mark has lived and worked in remote and often troubled parts of the globe including Rwanda and the African Great Lakes region. His permanent home is in Cheshire England, where he lives alone with a part-time lodger called depression and many full-time friends. He has been married twice and has four children and two grandchildren.

To my parents and my children.

Mark Bickerton

Day Return to Cocoa Yard

Anthology of novellas and short stories

AUSTIN MACAULEY PUBLISHERS™

LONDON • CAMBRIDGE • NEW YORK • SHARJAH

A CIP catalogue record for this title is available from the British Library.

ISBN 9781528990943 (Paperback)
ISBN 9781528990950 (ePub e-book)

www.austinmacauley.com

First Published (2020)
Austin Macauley Publishers Ltd
25 Canada Square
Canary Wharf
London
E14 5LQ

The author wishes to thank the Bickertons: Mary Madeline, Harry, El Gabriel, Dominic, Charlie, Constance, Paul, Gary and Terry, also Jayne, Miranda Gorst, Zoe, and all his friends especially Dave Turner, the Knappers and Chris Shenton, who are a bridge over troubled water. Thanks also go to the many characters good and evil encountered on his travels, who have—sometimes unwittingly—inspired these writings.

Table of Contents

"Repas Heureux"

Seventeen days after the bairn showed up in the world I was the happiest man alive. She was eight pound eleven ounces, a big baby that meant poor wee Danni had to be cut. I was there for the birth, dashed over from Clyde, and there for the needlework. The Chinese doctor with the thread had a cold and he was breathing hard, trying to sniff back the snot that was saturating his mask because he couldn't interrupt the flow of what he was doing to blow his nose, and I was sitting there worrying he'd infect us, especially the baby. Would I kick off about it? Tell them to send some other doctor without ailment? Still, these guys are snowed under and wee one was sleeping in her tantalus, smiling blissfully unaware, and despite my concerns about the doctor's germs, Danni and I couldn't stop smiling too, and whispering that we'd brought something so wonderful, miraculous, into this shitty world.

After two drunken days and nights I was back to the infirmary with my sister because she had a car to bring them home, mother and daughter. The little thing, that's my daughter not Danni, pink with tufts of hair, the tiny hands also pink and plump as I allowed her to grip my finger. Danni and I were nervous, anxious, inexperienced and excited twenty-something new parents to the wee bundle of miracles, her beautiful face creased as a fist. Phoebe was what we decided.

At the time I was welding on the Clyde in Govan, just about clinging to a job Thatcher's Eighties would surely claim. "Another wee belly to fill," Danni said. So between shifts at the pub with the lads to wet the bairn's head, I was putting in as much overtime as possible, welding the social, professional and fatherly roles together. Until with impeccable timing, calamity struck and I was told the job was no more

– come end of the month I'd be like the rest of the lads and the hordes of unwashed hopeless.

With Danni not working obviously we needed something quick but it wasn't easy. Precious few new ships to sail and my redundancy package such as it was would not last so long. So when my brother-in-law, Peter, said he needed a hand with a painting job, I tore his arm off from the pit.

"Guess who's got work?" I said to Danni who was giving wee Phoebe a bottle when I was in from the pub.

"Great!" she exclaimed, "Where?"

"Painting job with Pete," I said.

"Ah, that's brilliant so it is," she said, "But where?"

"Only temp, but it'll keep us going till I find something more permanent."

"Of course but are you going to tell me where?"

"He said we should be able to string this one out for a month or so."

"But where for Christ's sake?" she said. And I took a breath or two before saying the word.

Peter's friend of a friend of a friend called Fat Andy from Edinburgh was one man the eighties were being good to. He drove a fancy BMW and owned a string of properties from Edinburgh to London or beyond, and his latest acquisition was a Pyrenean chalet in some place called Les Angles near Andorra. Apparently, he bought it so him and his wife could spend the winter there skiing, jammy fat bastard, and he wanted it fixing up for their first trip to icy luxury.

"I've seen the photos," said Pete, "it looks fucking amazing."

"So what will we be doing?" I asked him.

"Apparently, the roof wants looking at, the drains are backing up and some of the wooden structure needs replacing."

"Sounds like a big job."

"Maybe a month and we'll need scaffolding. I'm taking you and a guy called Ab I met in the pub. Nice enough bloke with a wonky eye but knows his way around the tools. He's signing on and fancies a bit of moonlighting."

"So what will I be doing?" I asked.

"The balcony's away from the back wall in danger of coming down the mountain."

"She'll be comin' down the mountain when she comes."

"Aye," he said, unimpressed, "That's where you come in, with your welding gear."

"Brilliant."

"And then it wants repainting, inside and out, and the floor varnishing. That's where we *all* come in. Last job, we varnish our way out the door so it goes off when we close up behind us and say *au revoir*."

"Sounds great."

"Aye. There's a lake at the bottom of the mountain called Lac Matemale and you can see ibex apparently."

"Is that a fish?"

"No, it's a goat."

"In the lake?"

"Fuck off you prick. Do you want the job or not?"

"I want the job aye."

"I'll show you the plans tomorrow. Meantime, you'll have to work out how you're going to tell Danni you'll be leaving her and the wee bairn."

"No sweat," I said and hid a while in my pint as he gave me a look, before adding "I'll tell her it was Tebbit's orders."

And that night I found her giving my beautiful little Phoebe a bottle and nervously said the word.

"France?" she said, pulling the bottle out with a plop.

And so I told her the spec, all about Pete's friend of a friend of a friend called Fat Andy from Edinburgh who was doing well for himself in his posh BMW and string of properties the latest of which was some holiday retreat in the Pyrenees.

"Bully for him! But France!"

"I know, hen, but the man's a gold mine. Could be a lot more work if we pull this one off."

"What about me and wee Phoebe?"

"I know I know," I said, softly. "But the money won't last for ever. We need to feed wee one and clothe her, they soon grow out of things my sister said, and somewhere to live. She'll outgrow this place as quick as her clothes."

"I know," she said, showing signs of weakening.

"I'll phone every day," I said.

"You'd better."

"And Millie said she'd come round and help with wee one."

"You told your sister before you told me!"

"Only because I was nervous of telling you," I reassured, knowing I'd jeopardised things and fearing some fire from the Irish side of her.

"What did she say?"

"She said of course she'd help you, goes without saying. And she knows the score, we need the money."

"Is she all right with Pete going to France?"

"No sweat at all, she said. She trusts him."

"Are you saying I don't trust *you*?"

"I'm not saying that! I know you trust me. It's in the mountains, there'll be bugger all else to do except work."

"No French madams then?"

"No French madams I promise. Anyway, apparently there are ibex."

"What are ibex?"

"Goats. Would you mind if I got that desperate?"

And she laughed and said take over the feed because she needed a pee.

"Are you sure this fucking heap of rust will get us there?" asked Ab, giving Pete's old DAF the once-over with the eye that could find it.

"Cheeky bastard," said Pete, "This van's never let me down. Get your tools in."

Pete had got the cheapest deal possible and we were to drive to Dover for the ferry then share the driving from Calais through Paris, down through Limoges, Toulouse and climb the Pyrenees to Les Angles. He knew the route, got it sussed, and even knew where we'd be stopping off for a beer and a bite. It was a long trip but we were ready for it, excited, three

14

lads in a van, a bit of money in our pockets, singing songs. Ab even had his banjo, which he couldn't play but at least he had it. He seemed a decent bloke, bit of a joker, non-stop supplier of weed and simplistic views of life and how to handle women. "Treat 'em mean," he said, "let 'em know who's boss." Turned out he'd been married three times and hadn't even told his current wife he was coming for fear she'd say no. Just told her he was away for a pint. But he was tolerable except for his feet and the smelliest farts ever known to man – not what you want for a twelve-hour drive in a capsule as small as that and Pete often threatened to make him walk. But we survived it. Just.

By the time we got there, I was already missing Danni and the baby, so Pete dropped me in the village of Les Angles to find a phone box. It took me ages to get through because I didn't know you had to drop the first zero of the code till Ab put me right.

"Hiya, hen," I said.

"Hello, you!" she said, "I can hear you so clearly."

"Everything OK?"

"Never mind me, did you get there safely?"

"We did aye," I said, "How's my Phoebe?"

"Phoebe's fine," she said with a giggle, "and sleeping at last so I won't put her on if that's OK?"

"I'll not spend long on because of the money and Pete wants to get started," I said.

"No," she said, "And tell the bugger to pay you well."

"See you soon."

"A month feels like ages, make it a quick one."

"It won't when you're used to it. I'll phone every day."

"You'd better or the locks will be changed when you get back."

"I will," I said, "I will."

"Love you, hun," she said.

"You too, Danni."

"And leave those goats alone."

The chalet was a mostly timber construction, two A-frames carved into the cliff face and when you ventured inside, it was bigger than it seemed from the outside. A pyramidal Tardis. Downstairs there was a wee vestibule with a cupboard and toilet off, and the one large room with a log fire beyond had a kitchen niched into the corner. A large window at the far end looked out onto the most picturesque views I've ever known, down over the valley to Lac Matemale which seemed like a puddle from so far. We couldn't go out on the balcony yet because I could already see it was coming away, and one boot trodden on the wooden decking would've surely sent it, and us, tumbling down the mountain. The hills beyond were snow-capped, but just outside it was mostly dry, the odd patch of white here and there among the pines where buzzards soared and rested. Up some winding stairs off the living space were two fair-sized double bedrooms and a small cove to sleep one, which Ab bagsied and we were glad on account of his flatulence. As I set down my bag and tackle, Pete was already downstairs throwing logs on the fire to get it stoked – the place was cold and needed a good airing – then he'd set about his recce of the work we were there to do.

That night we sat thawing by the fire, eating baguettes with French ham, drinking five-centime bottles of wine we'd grabbed in Limoges, talking, joking and listening to Ab's farts and songs accompanied by his equally tuneless banjo. But then, before we settled merrily for the night, Pete dished out the rota, my first job being going down to the village to get some provisions and source the scaffolding before making a start on the balcony.

Which was no mean feat. Balanced precariously over the precipice, I knew there was hardly any footing before the big drop. But with a series of poles and ropes, I managed to climb up there and, well aware of the two hundred feet down, make a start on replacing brackets I'd welded and bolted below. It took a good three days to fix rigidly in place and Pete was pleased with the outcome, taking pictures to show Fat Andy when we got back.

"A fucking doddle," said Ab, casting his good eye over the fruits of my labour, "I'd have that done in half the time."

"Bollocks," I said, "You'd spend two days searching for the fucking thing with the one eye that works."

And we all laughed.

The job was a sound one, the main problem being the shit-filled drains which meant digging into hard rock outside and finding the source. At one point Pete pierced through the mains pipe and water spurted everywhere, so we had to dash down to the village and ask for a plumber who wore a wig. Reluctantly he came up the hill and gave us a hand, climbing into the sopping hole and turning the main key to shut off the supply. Guiltily, I handed him a beer to keep him going and he angrily cried, "*Apres le putain de boulot!*" We didn't know what it meant but it sounded rude so Ab said, "Keep your hair on!" and we fell about laughing while the poor oblivious bastard got his toupee drenched.

But that was the trickiest working day, the rest was a breeze, and by the time we got round to painting we could stretch things out, stretch our legs at times, explore the couple of bars in the village and get pissed on cheap French and Spanish wine. We even drove down to Perpignon for a taste of sea salt and sunshine, laughing at Ab's cack-handed chat-up lines to the bikini'd beauties, who weren't sure if he was talking to them or someone over their shoulder. I knew I was having the time of my life and though I missed Danni and Phoebe and kept my promise of phoning every day, it would be something I'd look back on with pride and tell my grand-kids. And by the time it came to say goodbye to the place, I felt saddened to miss its dreamy beauty, and even worse that I'd be going back to the harsh reality of the dole. I'd put a coat of varnish on my cold existence, that was all.

When I returned to our little one-bed flat in Govan, I found Danni waiting for me, a sign up in the window saying 'welcome home daddy'. I gave her the hardest hug of my life and asked where was the bairn and she was sleeping in her carry where I noticed the first tufts of hair turning orange from the Irish half of her mother. I wanted to pick her up and at first, Danni said no she hadn't been sleeping, then caved in. I'd missed them so much and while I'd had a good time in France, I was glad to be with the woman and daughter I loved the bones of.

Pete had paid me well for the work and first chance I got, I asked my sister to babysit while I took Danni out for a curry, though I had a bit of a fight because she said we needed to go careful. She ate hungrily, a veg *biriani*, saying she really wanted to win her figure back, and enjoying my Pyrenean stories about the plumber in the toupee and the drains that were backing up and reeked of shit. She was appreciating the rest from baby yet wanting to get to the phone every five minutes to check everything was OK. "Relax," I told her, "Everything's fine. Millie knows what she's doing. We're going to a club next."

"We're not," she said, firmly, "I told Millie we'd be back by twelve. We are not going to a club." And that was final, I knew it, no argument, so I squeezed her hand and said OK, hen, we'd be back straight after the meal and I loved her.

We were very happy, Danni and I and little baby Phoebe and though I had no work lined up as yet, it wasn't for lack of trying. I went round all the yards and asked if anything was going, and even trawled the local garages to ask for welding jobs, valeting even, anything. But nothing, and Danni kept saying keep trying because something was bound to come up.

When Phoebe was about one with all her teeth and toddling, it was Danni who found some cleaning work while I stayed at home. I was happy to be with baby, not self-conscious when out or walking the pushchair one-handed like other fathers did for fear of emasculation. I was happy. I loved spending time just me and baby. Now and then I used to watch her sleeping, the miraculous tiny rise and fall of a beating wee heart. And I was happy for Danni to bring in some money, buy herself some new clothes now she was slim again, she'd won her figure back, some independence. I couldn't wait for her to come home though, so I could tell her all about my day with Phoebe, how she'd said Dada again, and she could tell me all about her day, cleaning for Mrs Montague and Mr Wilson who had a son called Harry who'd always drop by to check up that his dad was getting his money's worth. Apparently, he played tuba in a brass band and once invited her to go and see them play but she'd said no.

"Why not?" I said.

"What do I know about brass bands?" she said.

"Hen, it'll do you good to get out."

So eventually she did, and got to quite like it, even talked about learning the trumpet one day and it made me laugh.

"What's so funny about that?" she said, "Harry said I could pick it up easily."

"Harry would," I said, "And anyway it's one thing picking it up another being able to play the bloody thing!"

Over the weeks to follow, Harry came to pick Danni up and go to see the band play as often as possible which I encouraged. I even met him a couple of times, seemed a nice enough fella.

"It's when a person stops talking about a person that you need to worry," said Millie, and I was stupid enough to ignore her. Because it was true, in hindsight, I noticed Danni would go off to these band practices and gradually stopped mentioning Harry by name, and he wasn't picking her up anymore; she'd get there under her own steam. And I thought nothing of it, till Ab saw me in the pub one night and happened to mention he saw my wife get into a bloke's car in Evans Street round the corner from our flat. "You want to keep that one on a lead," he said with a wink of the eye that could see me, and I told him to mind his own business, my wife was sound and he should fuck off back to his third. If anyone decided to keep an eye on her it was me. I was cool.

Till the night she told me her head had been turned and my heart got broken.

"What did he do to you?" I demanded to know.

"Nothing!" she said.

"What did he fucking do to you!"

"Don't shout, the baby's crying!"

"Danni, I want to know! If he's laid a single finger on you, I'll kill him! He'll need a fucking surgeon to get his tuba out of his arse!"

"He hasn't!" she screamed and broke down in tears, head in hands on the settee.

I didn't want to go and sit with her, I couldn't, I couldn't touch her right now, I guess for fear he had touched her, I'd be touching him. That sounds weird but how else can I describe how I felt? Angry? Betrayed? Scared, definitely that. I was scared of losing her.

"I'll tell you what happened," she sobbed, so I sat at the table, six feet away, shaking like the bottles of baby milk in front of me, waiting for her to tell me it was over, she was in love with someone else.

"Are you in love with him?"

"No," she said, "I'm not in love with him. It was nothing at first, he was just a bloke whose father I did for, who kept coming to check for cobwebs, check I was doing my job properly I told you. And then with the band thing, again it was just an interest and yes I got to kind of like it."

"And what about him?"

"Yes, I got to quite like him too. Not in that way."

"In what way?"

"In that way. He was just someone I saw as a friend, till the day when…"

"When what? Please, Danni, I want to know, I deserve to know."

"… I looked at him and thought he was actually quite attractive."

"Fucking hell I feel sick."

"And one night…"

"What? One night what?"

"He said he wanted to kiss me."

"Outside our house?"

"No. In the car near the bandstand."

There was a long pause that felt like an hour, and I'm still shaking, probably gone bloodless, feeling cold and dreading what was to follow.

"And did you?"

"No."

"You didn't kiss him?"

"No, I swear I didn't!"

"But you were tempted, is that it?"

"I don't know."

"Danni!"

"Don't shout, the baby's up!"

"I don't care! Tell me, were you fucking tempted?"

"Yes I was fucking tempted! But I didn't, I swear!"

I couldn't go on with that line of enquiry, so sick was I in the stomach. I just went to the bedroom and scooped the baby up, cuddling her, crying into her blanket, ruing the day I fucking encouraged her to go to watch his poxy band in the first place. When I finally got the baby back down, I found Danni making us a cup of tea, her back to me, and saying, "I won't be going there again. To band practice. I'll tell him."

"No," I said, "I will."

And that was it. We didn't mention it again. When I thought about it, I still felt sick, but tried not to show it, let it get to me. But these things fester I guess and it was hard. I was still unemployed and she'd be going out four days a week, cleaning, but not at Mr Wilson's, and I was there with Phoebe, and when it wasn't busy, when she was sleeping and I finally got to put my feet up in front of shit TV, exhausted, it kept coming back to me. I didn't know how to control it at times. Sometimes I'd kick the wall in anger and frustration, hurt and shame. Yes shame, because what man can neglect his wife so much she finds temptation? What kind of man was I, sitting there in front of shit TV, mixing Cow & Gate Plus? The man who hadn't done anything wrong, just doing his best for his wife and kid, who through no fault of his own had nothing else to do. Except drink.

Though Danni got home from work knackered, as much as possible I'd find a way of getting out to the pub, which at first she said I deserved after a busy day with the wee one. But gradually the odd night out with the lads became three or four times a week, then more than that, then most nights then every night, which of course became an issue. Danni knew that deep down I was punishing her for what she had or hadn't done, I sensed it. She didn't say it but it was in the air, hanging there behind every conversation, lurking eerily at the back of every minor disagreement, everything that caused a voice to rise. If there was any room at all in that cramped little tenement I sensed she'd grown to hate, there would be an elephant, and that man Harry and what she might or might not have done with him was it.

Though Danni didn't say much about my drinking at first, I know she told Millie about her concerns because Millie had a quiet word, telling me she'd no idea what was going on but something wasn't right, and drinking wouldn't help. But I didn't listen, so every night when Danni came home I'd be away for a pint, sometimes even before she'd got chance to tell me about her day. That was how it was, how it had become, and how it would be for the next four years when Phoebe was ready for school.

So I hadn't learned. And by the time Danni walked out on me and took my beautiful daughter, Phoebe, I was one fucked-up man. Unhappiest man in the world. She'd found herself someone new, from England some place and called George of all things. At first, she was fair you know with access, I got to see Phoebe on the weekend, take her to the park, to the pictures, McDonald's, all the things starving dads do. Then one day sometime later, Danni phoned to say would I mind missing one weekend because she and George were taking Phoebe to Disney Land Paris? Well, I was rocked. Disney Land, a place *I* always wanted to take her, now she was being taken by some fucker else! My instinct was to say no, fuck off, you can't do that, take my kid out of the country without my permission, but she said it was already booked so don't kick off. "You went to France that time and left me alone with the kid," she said with an exaggerated Gallic shrug, "Well, now it's our turn."

"It was work!" I said, "I went to France to clothe the wee one!"

"And now you're *not* clothing the wee one," she said, "You're on the dole like all the other wasters you drink with."

Those were the words that cut me, that would haunt me. But then, part of me thought what man could deny his little kid the chance of a lifetime, what man could do that? And anyway Danni said to make up for it I could have her for a whole week when they came back. So a couple of weeks later when I'd calmed down, I agreed and booked that week off work accordingly, because by then I'd managed to find something, just some labouring but it was something, it was finally something to restore a bit of dignity. But that didn't happen, I never got Phoebe for the whole week, because they never came back.

Turns out this George was some wine merchant and he'd bought a cottage in Bordeaux, and this whole Disney thing was a ruse for fuck's sake. Oh they did go there right enough, but what they didn't tell me was that from Paris it was on to the south where he'd be doing the business.

It's not easy to describe how I felt. Sick? Gutted? Betrayed? Broken-hearted? Angry? Suicidal? No, while I felt all of them, none of them can cut it, not even suicidal, none of those words can convey how a man feels when having his whole life smashed to pieces. I used the words fucked-up and I guess that just about does it. The week I took off work turned into two and three and four and so on, till in the end the doctor signed me off for a whole three months ongoing. He wanted to give me Valium but I refused, seen too many people hooked on that shit.

The other thing that's not easy to describe or even justify is what I did about it. I mean some say I should've fought tooth and nail to keep my beautiful little daughter in the country, found a lawyer, contested, what kind of man, what kind of father, could not? And I have to admit I set about doing all these things, once I'd dried my eyes, stopped kicking walls and demanding justice, but never quite followed them through; not because I didn't want to, more because I didn't have the energy so broken was my mind and body. Sure I was able to speak with Phoebe on the phone – Danni would call and put her on. Hearing her voice went some way to alleviate the pain, yet at the same time pushed the dagger further into my heart then twisted it. I was even invited over to see them, and once even bought the tickets, but that week I got laid off from the labouring job and my world completely caved in a second time. Danni accused me of letting Phoebe down. Me? Let my beautiful Phoebe down? I'd never do that, I said, I was ill, I couldn't make the trip, I lost my job, it's breaking my heart not to see her. It was the first sign of Danni, the woman I once loved, still loved, being a changed person and I didn't like it, it was another stab in my heart and another one-way street towards the bottle. What I was too mad and too stupid to know was that I was getting sicker and sicker.

Then, after a bloated sixteen weeks on the booze and not much else I don't know how it happened but I guess a light came on, when I woke up crying having dreamed of my little girl in France. I felt wretched, angry, hurt, a bile in my gut, yes all of those words, but something else was gnawing away at my consciousness – and it was seeing Phoebe laughing amid the vines, playing with her mummy, playing with other kids, going to school and picking up French. And I thought what kind of man could deny the little girl a dream of her own? Wasn't that a better life Danni could give her there? Wasn't that better than growing up in Glasgow, living with a daddy who was just an out of work welder and never quite getting it together to even take her to Euro-Disney? With a father who had a drink problem? That was the light bulb that went on in my head that made me see things including myself more clearly.

At that time the calls were still coming, but as Phoebe got older, they became gradually less and less and more and more painful in a way. Yet paradoxically in conjunction my life was on the up. I quit the booze, got clean, found a new job, got a new girlfriend called Alice who had work and rented an apartment in Shawlands. Alice was good for me and for once, I was good to myself. I enjoyed my job, it wasn't much, just some welding and stuff for a small private garage, but it was something and yes I liked it. With Alice's wage (she was a bank cashier) we could afford to live OK. Not rich by any stretch, just OK. As I say, she and I were good to me, I'd found a vital lifeline and was able to actually live. We got new friends, ate well, I even started jogging for Christ's sake. And again some men, especially the kind of men who dress as Batman and climb pylons and buildings in protest at not seeing their kids, would knock me for this, but I admit as time wore on the pain of not seeing Phoebe eased away. The resentment and images that once were so raw were less so. Of course I still got to speak to her, and via Alice's computer I also got to Skype, but the thought of never seeing her again in the flesh, not being able to touch her skin, put my arm around her and squeeze her, let her hold my hand like the day she was born, was less and less hurtful, less and less hard as I got on with my life. That's what some men would criticise me for, but that's how it was. Hang me.

So it was only via Skype that I saw her features change as time wore on, and it was only via Skype that she saw mine change too – much older and greyer than I should've been for my age, the hard times etched on my face, but still the sparkle in my eyes or so she said. And I got to watch her grow up like that and learn how she was doing at school, how she was now fluent in French.

*

I don't want to describe how it felt not to see my grand-child when it was born, not to be able to put my finger in its hand and let it gently squeeze, only to see it on a laptop screen, just to say it felt much like it felt when Phoebe was taken away from me all those years ago. Except maybe this time it wasn't Danni's fault, at least not directly. I say not directly because if she hadn't taken Phoebe away in the first place, I could've got to see my grandchild actually born. But once again, I was getting on with my life, hoping deep down or knowing it, that one day, one day, I *would* get to see them, Phoebe and Aline as she was called, my daughter and my granddaughter, in the flesh.

It happened, when it happened, out of the blue. Four years after the day I learned Phoebe was pregnant, four years pushing a broken heart to the back of my mind, my mobile suddenly rang. I say suddenly, don't phones always ring suddenly? I mean they don't take a run-up or give you a warning so you think "ah I've a funny feeling my phone is going to ring" or something ridiculous like that. Anyway, I was in the bath at the time so I jumped out and answered. And I heard Phoebe's voice. Not from Bordeaux, not from France at all, but from Scotland, in fact from Glasgow, in fact from the airport and would I pick them up? In fact, right now! Naked and dripping and shaking not from the cold but from shock and excitement, I said yes, sure I didn't need telling twice.

Luckily, Alice had a day off work and she said I could take the car. I asked if she wanted to come with me and though she knew I was kind of nervous I guess, and might need some support, she said it was best if I went alone. It's a family thing and I should have them all to myself. All in good time, she said, with a smile I hadn't seen before, that was somehow different, she would get to meet my daughter and granddaughter. And then it struck me, I didn't even know how long they were staying or even *if* they were staying. But I didn't need to dwell on that, because Alice had said those words. My daughter and granddaughter. I asked her to say it again. My daughter and granddaughter.

It was less than ten miles from where we lived to the airport and I drove like a lunatic. Not because I drive like a lunatic, but because I was so nervous. I overtook badly once and got a one-finger salute from some arsehole in an Audi, and though I gave him one back, I told myself to calm down, slow down. But it wasn't easy. I was thinking how long it was since I saw her, how long it was since I touched her face, Phoebe, my beautiful daughter. I'd seen her on Alice's laptop enough times to know what she looked like now, it would be wrong to say otherwise – her long red hair, her freckles, her beautiful eyes darker than usual for a redhead, in fact blue, a rarity, which helped make her the beautiful, unique girl she was, the beautiful, unique woman she now was. I'd also seen my granddaughter, wee Aline, right there on Skype, darker, more like her father Jean maybe, dark eyes like lakes looking back at me and smiling so I wanted to reach into the screen and dive into them. But that wasn't possible. Not until today.

It was a KLM flight and delayed by nearly an hour, but I didn't care as I waited in Arrivals because though it would mean one hour less with them, as precious as every moment was, it gave me time to think what would I say? What would I do? Would I give her a massive hug? Of course, I would. But who first? Phoebe? Or would I first grab hold of my granddaughter, pick her up and throw her into the air? Finally, I decided I'd let things just happen, not rehearse what to say or do, just let things happen.

And finally, there they were. I first saw Phoebe and her beautiful red hair turned gold in the concourse light, pushing a trolley full of cases with her right hand and, in her left, this toddler wearing a little hat, a little coat, little gloves and black and white pumps, taking her first tiny steps into her homeland.

So I'll tell you what did happen, I ran towards them and pulled Phoebe away from the trolley, scooped her up in my arms and gave her the hardest kiss of my life, then almost in the same movement I crouched down to the little one and did the same to her. And then the same, twice over and twice as hard. Once again I have difficulty describing how I felt; elated? Overjoyed? The happiest man in the world? Probably all of those but definitely the last.

"*Bonjour*, Papa," said Phoebe.

"*Bonjour, mon petite fille*," I said.

"Wow," said Phoebe, "Full marks!"

"I've been practising," I said.

I can't honestly remember how long we stood there exchanging words and hugging and everything, probably ten minutes who knows? But I wouldn't care if it were an hour, I was so desperate to look into their eyes, the blue and the black, keep hugging them, talking to them in English, bad French and utter shite. It didn't matter, it just didn't matter, because there I was, with my daughter and my granddaughter, my beautiful daughter Phoebe now a grown woman and my little darling Aline.

"Good flight?" I said at last, "You must be starving!"

"A bit," said Phoebe.

"Are you hungry, little one?" I said.

"*Oui*," said Aline, then remembering it was to be English, just nodded, and hid behind her mother's coat.

I don't remember much of what I said on the drive towards the city but the journey seemed to take just minutes, and it didn't seem long before we'd found a McDonald's in Argyle Street, ordered up and taken a seat in the window. And again I must've been talking garrulous as a budgie, as if packing as much as I could into the time it took to say a medium fries, so keen was I to fill in the gaps, so desperate was I to gobble them up while I had them there in front of me.

"Slow down, Dad," said Phoebe, "there's no rush."

"Well, this morning when I talked to Alice, that's my girlfriend…"

"… I know."

"… it occurred to me I hadn't even asked how long you were staying, *where* you were staying! I mean if this is a flying visit, I want to make the most of you."

"It's OK, Dad," she said, "We're here for a week."

A week! A week that felt like eternity ahead of me, a time in which to get these two beautiful people back into my life.

"Have you got a hotel?" I asked.

"Not yet," she said.

"Well, listen, feel free to say no if it's too much or too soon, but I'd love it if you came to stay with us?"

"Really?" she said, with a smile I'd never seen before.

"Really," I said, "and don't worry about Alice because she'll be fine with it. She's already said."

"Are you sure?"

"Positive," I confirmed, "I've never been more positive about anything in my life."

"*Oui*," said Aline, who by now had overcome her shyness and was greedily devouring her fries and added, "I want to stay with Grandpapa."

To hear her say that, grandpapa, made my heart dance.

"She has a good appetite," I said.

"She'll eat you out of house and home," said Phoebe.

"I don't care. She can have anything she wants."

"She's ever so bright, Dad."

"I can see that. Two languages. She's very lucky to have a mum like you."

"So am I," said Phoebe, "To have a dad like you. I've missed you so much."

And so that was the first meal I ever had with my granddaughter, and the first time I'd seen my daughter in too many years that I care to mention. And I'd got them for a whole week. I couldn't help thinking the last time I saw her was before Danni promised I could have her for a week after they'd returned from Disney Land Paris and they never did. But I didn't want to dwell on that. I didn't want to dwell on anything negative, just enjoy that week, those moments, that laughter, those stories they'd tell, and lap them up and squeeze them dry for everything I could. I was the happiest man in the world having a happy meal, *repas heureux* said wee Aline, thinking of the week ahead of us and what to make of it.

But knowing me as I do, I'd be trying to wring out as much as I could from that week while growing increasingly aware of the clock ticking towards that time when I'd have to say goodbye all over again to my beautiful daughter and granddaughter. So imagine how it felt when I learned that one week was to become forever! When we arrived at my home, Alice was ready with a poster in the front window, in French!
– *Bienvenue Phoebe et Aline!*

"You knew they were coming here?" I said.

"I did aye," Alice confessed, with the same smile I'd seen earlier that day and didn't recognise.

"Sorry, Dad," said Phoebe, "I kept it secret that I'd phoned ahead."

"But I don't get it," I said, looking from Alice to Phoebe and back with a face I'm sure screwed up in confusion.

"Thing is," said Phoebe, "I left Jean, you know. We're home, Dad. For good. I want us to see Mum as well. It's been too long. I want us to make a life here."

The news engulfed me with joy, happiness, elation, all of those words wrapped up in one bountiful emotion. There I was with these three beautiful women of my life about to make it more complete than it'd been for years.

"That's if you want us," she said.

"Oh I want you," I said, scooping wee Aline up in my arms and swinging her around to make her giggle.

"We will go back to France every so often," she said, "It's important wee one gets to see her daddy."

"Aye," I agreed, "I feel very strongly about that. Though I never dressed as Batman and never climbed a single pylon!"

"I know," she said, "But we're here now."

"I can't tell you how that feels," I said, "Can I ask one wee favour?"

"What?"

"This might sound stupid."

"What?"

"Please will you hold my hand like the day you were born?"

And she did. And this time I knew I'd never let her go.

*

"The Sleeper on the Train"

Him.

On Tottenham Court Road he walked north to Euston and spotted something gleaming gold on the pavement. At first he thought it could be valuable. But as he stooped to pick it up, he saw it was an earring, and on closer inspection that it was not in fact real gold. So he pocketed the tiny sleeper, no bigger in circumference or more valuable than a five pence piece, thinking instead it could be a sign, some blingy portent of better things to come for a man down on his luck.

One hour later, he was on a train waiting for it to take him back to where he needed to be, which happened to be Manchester. Just as the train was about to move, a woman embarked and chose a seat opposite. She was hot, flustered, in a state of panic. She had lots of luggage and he, being a gentleman, offered assistance.

"Thank you," she said with beaded brow, "you're very kind." And the traveller saw that she was beautiful, with blonde hair thick and wavy, offering the tousled look of a day in London, blue eyes and, as she struggled free of her leather jacket he saw that she was slim.

"You only just made it," he said.

"Yea," she replied, tucking her hair behind an ear with nails painted like pearls. "And I'm bound to have forgotten something. I always seem to leave something behind, everywhere I go, because I'm always running late."

"Better late than never," he said, then kicked himself for such a hackneyed gambit, though she didn't seem to mind.

At last she was organised enough to take her seat opposite him, and as the train smoothly pulled away she reached into her handbag and took out a book, which he was delighted to note was one of his. Would he say so? he asked himself. Would it be considered self-congratulatory, or even a lie to curry favour? Or what if she said the back cover was too far from the front? That like chewing gum it started well then lost its flavour and went on forever and left a nasty taste? And she'd be leaving it behind like a ragged Metro for someone else to thumb? Something bad like that had happened once when he asked his partner Carol what she thought of chapter 1 of his latest work, a novel called *First Boots*.

"So what do you think?" he'd asked eagerly.

"In a word," she'd said, "shit. Nothing happened."

So no, he'd learned to keep these things to himself. Yet every now and then he couldn't help glancing across, scrutinising the woman's face for the merest tic of enjoyment. Was that a smile? Was that furrowed brow because she felt the pain of Harry, the protagonist who drove a bus and was now terminally ill? Did one of her family have Alzheimer's? Her father perhaps? Her mother? Once, she caught him glancing up and he averted his eye but not quite quick enough.

"Sorry," he said.

"That's OK," she replied and smiled invitingly.

"It's just it looks interesting. The book."

"Very actually."

"Good," he said compulsively.

She looked puzzled and he realised his comment must appear rather odd. Should he now qualify, say he was glad because he was the author?

"Got it for the journey," she explained.

"Were you in London on business?" he wanted to know, thinking maybe she was a publisher or literary agent because serendipity was his favourite word.

"Visiting a friend," she said, "She walked back with me to the station. A long walk but I hate the tube and anyway the weather's nice. And we kept stopping to browse in shops."

"And in one you bought the book."

"Waterstones," she said, and this would've been his cue to say he was glad because it was his, and how proud he was that the fruits of his imagination had made it to such an esteemed market. But suddenly she put the book down, slid back in her seat and closed her eyes. She was ready to nod off, she said, as much to herself as to him. And so his moment was gone.

He watched her sleep and she slept a long time, rocking occasionally to the rhythm of the rails. He wanted her to wake up, to continue their conversation. Would he 'accidentally' wake her by leaving his seat, or coughing or something? But how could he? How could he wake this beautiful woman who needed her sleep? What right had he to expect her to even *want* to go on talking to him, a complete stranger, even if she *had* known he was the author of the tale she was reading? And what right had he to feel a twinge of irritation that she'd now chosen sleep over the thing she said was interesting and very actually?

And then, her head tilted towards the window and, still sleeping, she pushed her blonde hair behind her ear again, and he saw that it was pierced but there was no earring in it, just a tiny hole. He'd already noticed the other ear when she sat down after he helped put her bags on the luggage rail above and she'd thanked him and mopped her beaded brow, but not till now did he realise it had a sleeper identical to the one he'd picked up on Tottenham Court Road, the one that still lay in his pocket and could be an omen. Could it really be hers? Could it really be the one she'd lost? The thing she'd left behind? There was a story in this. Serendipity.

He reached inside his pocket, found the tiny piece of bling and fished it out with his little finger, not even knowing yet what he was going to do. Was he going to wake her and say she'd lost it while she slept? That would sound implausible. Would he wait for her to wake and say he'd found it on the floor? He didn't know but needed to decide because the train was nearing where he needed to be which happened to be Manchester.

Her.

It was sometime later when suddenly she woke. Blinking into focus, she realised the man opposite had left his seat. She wondered how long she'd slept and, checking her phone, was surprised to see it was almost two hours. Pity, because the guy opposite was kind of cute, handsome actually, very friendly, a gentleman to whom she would've liked to talk more. She smiled to herself, picturing herself phoning her friend Jude to say she'd arrived home safely and had been talking to an interesting and handsome man on the train, like she was Celia Johnson or something. She knew her friend would ask if she got his number and she'd say no. Yea pity. Still, she felt better now for sleep and decided to press on with her book. As she opened it, something slid from its pages along with a handwritten note:

I think you might've lost this but I didn't want to wake you. I'm glad you like my book.

Kind regards,
M

*

"Your problem is you're not getting enough sex," Jude said to Michelle.

"Is that right?" said Michelle.

"No, it is not right. You have everything – rich husband, nice house, brand-new car sitting right there in the driveway, kids all fledged – but you're bored. It is not right, Michelle, it is not right at all."

They were on a table outside a bistro in Covent Garden, where they'd eaten paninis in the sun and were now having a bottle of wine. Jude, Michelle's American friend she knew from college, was smoking and offering morsels of advice between puffs.

"That's what I'm talking about, Michelle. Sure you need an outlet, and I'm not talking about watching mind-numbing soaps on TV or joining a fucking zumba class."

"An outlet," said Michelle, "You're saying sex is an outlet?"

"I sure am," said Jude, trumpeting smoke into the sunny air and emphatically crushing her third cigarette into the ashtray.

The fact that the two of them had ended up arguing over this, even to the point of vowing to end their volatile thirty-year friendship, and that the argument went on all the way to Euston, in and out of shops including Waterstones, and nearly made Michelle miss her train, doesn't matter. What matters to this story is that though Michelle joined the train in a state of anger and panic, she would later close her eyes and go to sleep for nearly two hours, and wake to the realisation that in her direct, American and brutal way, Jude had hit the nail on the head. And hit it, in her direct, American and brutal way, with a sledgehammer.

"May I help with your luggage?" the man had said, and she'd agreed, and said that she was grateful and he was very kind. And they'd talked a little, small-talk, about her propensity for lateness and leaving things behind, and about the nice weather that summer and about the book that she was reading. The thing she opened after sleeping to find an earring and a note to say he was glad she was enjoying his book.

His book! The book she was reading was written by that man, the man she thought was kind of cute, handsome actually, who helped lift her bags onto the luggage rail, who she'd caught glancing at her while she was reading, clearly to see if she was engaging with the story! What are the chances of this happening? What's more, *why* did this happen?

The sleeper that fell out of the book did not in fact belong to her – she'd taken it out because her earlobe was sore, probably down to the ear-bashing she'd taken from Jude! No, the earring wasn't hers, but the fact that it was identical to the one on the right side, the one she left in, was once again perhaps some kind of miracle, or a sign that he was taking an interest in her. A coincidence at the very least. It was a pity, she thought, that she never got to explain this to the man, and to thank him for his kindness, and to comment on the remarkable coincidence that she was reading *Cocoa Yard* which the man himself had penned!

"How was London?" Stephen asked when she got home later that night.

"It was lovely," she said, going on to describe her two-day break, which took in a show in the West End, a pleasant boat ride down the Thames and lots and lots of shopping.

"And how's Jude?" he asked.

"Fine," she said, saying nothing about their fight, "She sends her love."

"I hope you're hungry," he said, "dinner's nearly ready."

And he gave her a hug and she hugged him back – the man to whom she'd been married for thirty years, with whom she'd raised three children, now grown up with family of their own. The man she'd loved for all those years, ever since they met at a nightclub in Glasgow, who'd asked her to dance…

They had sex that night, after the bolognaise he'd cooked, which she'd said was nice, and after that she'd told him more about London and fallen asleep doing so, unaware that he was watching her sleep and wishing they could talk a bit more.

Stephen had already left for work when she woke next morning, but had taken the trouble as always to put out a cup for her morning tea, along with a tulip picked from their garden and a note to say he loved her. She read the note and smiled, but then remembered there was another note in her handbag, from the man on the train, the man who was kind and had written the book that she would put her feet up with and finish today, using the note as a bookmark whenever she broke for something to eat or drink.

It was a lovely story: moving, humorous and thought-provoking and when she read the final page, she put it down with some regret and cried.

It was now four in the afternoon and she knew it was time to start prepping dinner for when Stephen got home at seven. He worked so hard, she thought, and she deeply appreciated it, along with the nice house, the garden with the tulips, a brand-new car and everything that went with it. Yes, she loved the man, and yet today there was somehow something boring into her psyche. So as she took the rice from the cupboard and left it to soak, and began to mix the spices for the curry, she got to thinking about what that was. Was it that she hadn't made every effort to please him in bed the night before? Was it that she'd fallen asleep too soon afterwards, he did so love his pillow-talk? Or was it that in her heart of hearts she knew that she'd been having sex with him out of duty for a very long time? She gave this last question some thought and couldn't help reflecting that when they met as teenagers, she so valued his gorgeous friendship that she left it much longer to have sex with him than her friends left it with *their* boy-friends. *And why was that?* she asked herself. It was because she didn't want it to sully what they had together, to tarnish their friendship. And it was because she finally let him do it as that's what was expected rather than what she wanted, and what he'd been expecting and she hadn't always been wanting ever since. So ironically she let him do it because she feared *losing* his friendship if she didn't.

So Jude was wrong, she decided, about sex. Yes, she'd hit the nail on the head that Michelle was bored, but it wasn't sex she was needing, it was the freshness and excitement of a brand-new friendship. To find someone interesting and new to her, someone with new things to say, exciting opportunities to bring, unfamiliar places to see. She needed a key-change in her life to provide surprise, like how a good piece of music can change everything with a change of key. And yet, she thought, there was a strange stirring somewhere within her when she woke to find the man on the train had gone. She didn't know quite what it was, but it was something, and it was not unpleasant. And it was something strong enough to make her google his name, to discover who was his agent, and to write a letter in the hope that it would somehow reach him…

Dear Sir,

I am writing to thank you so much for your kindness on the train the other day and for your note. It is truly amazing that I happened to be reading your book I did wonder why you were paying so much interest! Imagine my surprise when it turned out I was sitting right opposite the author!

Thank you also for the earring however while I would've quite liked it to have been mine (that would've been another amazing story!) I have to say that it didn't belong to me. Nevertheless it was very kind of you to think of me and what an ingenious way of returning it in the pages of your book! Talking of which I finished it today and thoroughly enjoyed it – sadly my mother had Alzheimer's so I know how it feels to watch someone close die in such a horridly tragic way. Your words touched me and though they made me cry they also made me laugh out loud. So thank you once again.

Anyway I do hope this reaches you and you don't think I'm a stalker for researching and finding you via your agent.

Yours sincerely
Michelle Firth (the sleeper on the train).

The instant this plopped into the letterbox, Michelle regretted what she'd done. She almost wanted to reach in and claw the thing back out again. Or would she wait for someone to come and empty the box and plead with them to let her take it back? Of course they wouldn't be allowed to do that but she could own up that it was fanmail and she feels rather foolish, like she did when she wrote to Donny Osmond in the Seventies and was still waiting for his reply? Or she could lie that she'd sent it to the wrong person and it'd create all sorts of horrid problems that didn't bear thinking about? Or, she could tell the truth and say one of two things. Namely, she was embarrassed to have opened her heart to a writer who can describe emotions far more profoundly than her so she hopes he never receives it, like Donny Osmond clearly didn't. Or that she was thinking of her husband Stephen whom she loves but hopes the other man *does* receive it…and he *does* call the mobile number she'd written on the back?

*

Him.

"So…" said Carol and grimaced.

"So what?" said Mark abstractedly.

"So why do people start every sentence with the word 'So'?"

"I've no idea," he said.

She was sifting through the mail while he was reading the Guardian as per their breakfast routine.

"Two here from your agent," she went on. "Listen to this. "So I read your novel *Return to Cocoa Yard* and enjoyed it very much." He goes on to say nice things but why must he begin with 'So'? He does so more than once."

"At least he goes on to say nice things, that's the main thing," said Mark, hoping this would put the matter to bed but fearing Carol was now getting warmed up. The fact he agreed with her about the overuse of the word so was irrelevant, because like many things she said he was sick of hearing it and therefore loathe to encourage further discussion.

"It's like Irene at school," she said, "'So I went to buy a new dress at the weekend,' 'So I'm trying on this nice flowery number in Debenhams…' It's so fucking irritating."

"I know. So fucking irritating."

"And as for upward inflection don't get me started!"

"I won't," he said.

"I mean why must every sentence sound like a question? I'm not stupid, I do understand things, why can't it be a statement rather than a suggestion implying I don't understand?"

"Beats me."

"It doesn't beat me, it's another fucking import from America that people here think is a must-have."

"Point of fact I think upward inflection was invented in Australia," he said, finishing his coffee and rising to get another.

"Whatever," she perorated, "It's fucking irritating and pretentious."

Pretentious. It was one of her favourite words and it was mostly at breakfast when she was going through the mail that it tended to surface.

Mark flicked on the kettle and stared through the kitchen window at the world outside, thinking it was time he mowed the lawn, a job he hated, not so much the doing it but more the dodging cat shit and coiling up the cable and putting everything away in the shed with the spiders. The thought irked him and he was irked at being irked, like he was irked at himself for asking Carol to go through his mail in the first place. It was two years ago when his career was going well, and he'd asked her to be his kind-of secretary, partly because he felt he needed one and partly to supplement her income as a classroom assistant and he could put it down to tax. Yes, things were on the up in those days, in his career and in their relationship. At one time there was even talk of marriage but this was something they never got round to, much, he now realised, to his private relief. The job he'd invented for her mainly entailed opening his correspondence with his agent, dealing with fanmail (as he liked to term it although she probably thought that was 'pretentious') or missives from the ALCS or Writers' Guild, but had somehow and with no protestations from him developed into opening other items of mail besides those appertaining to his work. As he stirred his cup, he checked the kitchen clock and saw it was still half an hour before she left for work and he could get on with his writing. The realisation caused him to agitate the coffee more vigorously and almost clatter the spoon into the sink.

"This one's interesting though," she said, as he returned to the table with his replenished cup. "From a lady called Michelle whom you met on a train."

For reasons he'd only later rationalise, Mark knew straight away who the lady was but knew also that he had to pretend to the contrary. "A lady I met on a train?"

"She says you were very kind to her, helping her with her bags and whatnot, and it turns out she's reading your book."

"Ah. Yes, I remember. I didn't know she was called Michelle."

"Michelle Firth," said Carol.

"Right," said Mark, knowing and fearing what was coming.

"So what's this about you writing her a note?"

This was yet another of the many occasions where Mark somehow found himself on the back foot, knowing the truth was the best option but feeling the compulsion to lie because the truth would always be construed as damning. He knew he hadn't done anything wrong bar perhaps feeling sorry that the lady on the train fell asleep when he'd rather they continued to talk, but there was this awkward feeling that the omission of that detail would inevitably fester in Carol's mind and betray him in some way. Nowadays, he reflected, it seemed that everything however innocent would turn into a can of worms he'd have to wriggle his way out of. And so, while knowing Carol would sense instinctively that he was leaving something out, Mark began to explain that he was on the train after a successful talk on 'The Art of Storytelling' when a lady took the seat opposite and was flustered and panicked having only just made it before the train left, and he helped her put her luggage on the rail, and they'd got talking a little and he realised she was reading his book. As for the note, he explained, he saw she'd lost an earring and didn't want to wake her so placed it in the book.

"Seems a strange thing to do," Carol said.

"I know," he said, "But like I say, I didn't want to wake her, nor did I want to come straight out with it that I was the author of the book she was reading and how that was such a coincidence. That's all there is to it. Although I can't deny it was gratifying. I mean she might've said it was shit."

Carol didn't register the slight dig. "So, what did you say?" she asked, "In the note?"

"Nothing. I just said what I said to you, I didn't want to wake her and PS I was glad she was enjoying my book. That's all. To have *said* it was my book would've I think been egotistical, don't you?"

41

Her too.

When Carol arrived at work, she was met in the staff room as usual by the teaching fraternity, all psyching up for the day ahead and swapping stories about hormonal teenagers and their simple desire to just get through the day unscathed. Pete Threadgold, English, wanted Carol to help him with some writing exercise for his Year 11 group and while he explained his plan she listened and nodded appropriately, trying to shrug off what was really focusing her mind.

"That's all," Mark had said. He'd merely helped the woman with her bags and made small talk before noticing she was reading his book and he hadn't wanted to be egotistical so had left a note before getting off the train. On the surface, she supposed, that made sense, but there was something sub-textual going on, not least that he'd put a note in the book while she slept, which however you looked at it seemed slightly incongruous and even invasive. He'd actually *touched* her book, he'd actually picked it up and put a note inside along with the earring. It just didn't sit right. In her mind or at least in the way her mind was working it right now, touching the book was touching *her*.

"Everything OK?" asked Pete, seeing she was elsewhere.

"Fine," she said, but as they left the staff room and headed down the corridor to Year 11 she knew that her use of that word was nothing but perfunctory.

Their relationship was faltering. They'd begun so happily back then, indulging their shared passion for motorbikes, music and travel. It was only three months in when they were booking their first city break to Tallinn, for no other reason than he'd said it was somewhere he wanted to tick off. After that, they'd ticked off Vienna, Helsinki, Amsterdam, Copenhagen, Paris, Moscow and in fact most of Europe before venturing further afield and going long-haul to Nassau, New York and Florida. It was in Florida when she'd looked over her gin and tonic at the man in front of her, tanned and handsome, and marriage was mooted, and she'd bought him flowers because he'd said he'd always wanted to receive flowers yet women don't send them to men in general. She'd also bought him an encyclopaedia to help him with his writing and he'd pressed one of the flowers therein, on the page that contained the words Florida and Flower. A red rose, which was still there but now flat and beige as a biscuit, brittle enough to crumble in her hand. She'd checked. And in checking it had occurred to her that in the age of the internet things like encyclopaedias existed only on shelves and the art of flower-pressing was sadly all-but dead.

The wedding, of course, never happened, and she'd often wished she'd pressed him on the idea because what was proposed in a drunkenly happy moment in Miami was talked about in the days to follow, but time gradually sobered up and nothing concrete got ledgered. And as the weeks and months and years passed, it inevitably got forgotten altogether, even though they'd bought a house and lived and often laughed in it.

And then there was sex. It used to be so wonderful, he did things to her that she'd never known before. She'd had lots of sexual encounters before Mark, but none of them were anything to write home about and indeed some of them she deeply regretted. With Mark it was something she'd never regret and always enjoyed. Lately, however, he'd seemed somewhat distracted, which couldn't always be put down to his depression.

And she knew he masturbated. He didn't know she knew but she'd seen the evidence. She'd never asked him about it. She'd always wanted to but resisted for fear of the next question being whom he was thinking of when he was doing it? It wasn't her, she suspected. So who was it? Who was he thinking of *today*? The sleeper on the train as she pretentiously called herself? With this dreadful thought in her mind, and knowing she'd deftly filed the letter away and deliberately omitted to say that while there was no address on the letter, there was a mobile number written on the reverse, she entered the classroom with Pete and fashioned a smile for bloody Year 11.

Him.

Mark had taken his fourth coffee of the morning up to the spare room where he wrote. He'd opened his laptop and a Kit-Kat and prepared to write. But nothing came, and now, three hours later, he realised he hadn't written a single word. Frustrated and inexplicably angry, he pushed back his chair, put his hands behind his head and yawned. Why had his life gone tits-up? Two years ago, he was doing OK, selling his books and making a decent living. But then he'd had his breakdown, for no discernible reason he just began to spiral, the feeling of bleakness pervading, the utter despair that came from nowhere binding his ankles and dragging him down to untold depths like a dead weight. Carol had been understanding and he was grateful for that, and eventually agreed to see a doctor. She'd gone along with him for his first appointment, for support, and again he appreciated it.

Doggedly, he'd taken the anti-depressants the doctor doled out and sure, after a few weeks the symptoms abated, yet somehow and inexplicably the dog remained and resurfaced occasionally, and at the same time bred the awful dissatisfaction with his life and the inability to write anything of substance after *Day Return to Cocoa Yard*. And dissatisfaction with Carol too. The more concerned she became, the more irritated he was and the more insecure she became. He knew it but couldn't help it. And now, this morning, he had an awful feeling there was another episode coming his way, an episode in which he lacked belief in his writing, belief in himself and belief in their relationship.

He gazed despondently out of the window, which looked down on the same scene as that from the kitchen downstairs. He grimaced at the bad haircut that claimed to be a lawn – bald patches from the long dry summer but now sodden from recent downpours. Knowing he ought to replace this moment of procrastination with something useful like mowing it, he decided instead to masturbate. While doing that, he could feel good about himself, or feel that someone, and not Carol, felt good about him.

When he'd finished and destroyed the evidence in the way he'd come to believe water-tight, he went back to his desk intending to put down his thoughts. But only now did he realise there was something different permeating them today, and before too long he was going downstairs to look in the drawer where Carol filed his mail.

He took out the letter and read it for the first time then read it again, knowing he was searching for something between the lines. But there was nothing, he feared. Until just as he was going to file it back, he finally turned over the page and saw the mobile number the sleeper on the train had written. The sleeper on the train he wanted to wake up to keep talking. The sleeper on the train who had taken in the words of his book and taken her place in his fantasy.

"So…" he said and smiled.

Mark knew that one day he would call or text it. He wanted that thought to inspire him in some way, excite him even. But instead he found himself frustrated, because he knew Michelle lived probably miles and miles away and whatever he'd try to make happen would not happen right now, when he most needed something more in his life than writing or masturbating or mowing that fucking lawn or prepping dinner for when Carol got home from the school. In short, he was bored and frustrated. And where exactly did she live, the beautiful Michelle, with her long blonde seductive hair and one ear missing its bling, and her bright blue eyes and cheekbones like small apples? All he knew was that he'd left the train at Manchester and she'd remained on it, he'd seen her through the window as he headed for the exit at Piccadilly's Platform 14, and he'd seen she was seemingly still sleeping, and might've gone on sleeping all the way to Glasgow for all he knew.

So if he called that number right now, what could that *achieve* right now when he needed immediate excitement, distraction from the boredom and depression that purported to be his fifty-year-old life? Inevitably and unavoidably the thought turned his frustration into anger, and the thought of that lawn and its embedded cat shit could only exacerbate the issue and culminate in loathing; of cats, of a relationship he wanted out of, and of himself for his selfish depression. Just as he prepared to put his thoughts into words on the laptop screen, he looked down on to the lawn, where with sickeningly impeccable timing the neighbour's tomcat with its ludicrous name of Derek squatted to put down its fucking faecal traffic cone. Nauseous, Mark felt compelled to channel his ire into verse…

Cats gate crash my garden
Shit then split quiet as mice
It's not nice.
To say how I feel about felines
Who haven't even the courtesy
To bury their turds I'm lost for words.
And they eat birds.
Why should I go out to clear its dump with a clump of kitchen tissue
when the mouse-hound avoids the issue?
A friend of mine in Hitchin
provides a bog for his mog in the kitchen
Of all places.
I hate these faeces to pieces.

Having typed thunderingly, and called it Cat Doggerel for Bad Poetry Day, Mark dragged his seat back, finished his Kit Kat, and looked into the garden where Derek was now padding away with empty bowels.

"Well, Carol, that really *is* what you call shit!" he said aloud and instantly hit delete before adding, "What the fuck am I doing with my life?"

*

Her.
It was Saturday morning when Michelle received the call.

She was up early at the kitchen table, her tablet in front of her, dabbing her finger into various recipes from the internet. Stephen had dropped it on her late last night, when he came home from work, that he'd invited his co-director Ian Probin and his wife Steph for dinner. It was one of those ominous sentences that began: "I know it's short notice but…"

"But you know I hate dinner parties!" she'd protested, "I hate even the *idea* of dinner parties!"

"I'm sure you'd like them if you tried," he'd asserted.

"I won't. I know I won't."

"But you do like the Probins."

"I like Ed Sheeran but that doesn't mean I have to cook dinner for him."

"Now you're being silly," he said, "Anyway, you've never even been to a dinner party so how do you know you won't like them?"

That comment had hurt. Its implication that he was from better-heeled stock dug deep, like it always had down the years they'd been together. But she didn't address it, she never had, she'd always let it sink deep and rest on the soft bed of her feelings with all the others.

"But it's such short notice," was all she'd said.

"I agree, but at least it's Saturday and I won't be working for a change, so I can lend a hand, peel a few spuds or whatever."

"But what will I cook?"

"They're both meat-eaters so they're not fussy, though Steph doesn't like curry."

Fussy. He was fond of saying that of vegetarianism, itself another disparagement of her, from the day she'd turned semi-vegetarian twenty years ago, till now. To him it didn't make sense, especially as it meant doing two meals every night, though admittedly she did have the time with not working.

"Now I think I'll turn in if you don't mind. Been a knackering week."

And that, she knew, was that. No point arguing. Taken as read, like it was taken as read that he was the breadwinner, the man responsible for everything she had, the nice house and all its stylish furnishings, the garden with the tulips and the lovely car in the drive. So now she was at the kitchen table with the tablet, looking through recipes for anything other than curry while Stephen was still in bed for his customary Saturday morning lie-in.

Since she sent the letter, she'd done her best to forget about the man on the train. She'd felt foolish and regretful, and yet had her doubts as to whether the thing had even *reached* its intended recipient. Even if it had, how could she of all people expect a response? What a stupid thing to do to put her number on the back! At most she should've put her address on it, but hadn't done so lest Stephen opened any reply. And what the hell was she doing thinking he'd've written back anyway! But then that was another indication of her childishness, wanting the immediacy of response that texts these days offer, rather than the old-fashioned letters that made you wait like Donny did. Oh it was all so silly! Stephen was right, she *was* silly, a stupid, silly fifty-year-old woman who should know her place is to cook dinner for Stephen's important colleagues, appreciate and enjoy the comfortable life she'd been afforded, love the man she'd loved all these years, stop thinking stupid silly thoughts and take him up his cup of tea and breakfast. It was all Jude's fault with her brash American utterances about needing an outlet which led to their catfighting all the way from Covent Garden to Euston, including in Waterstones where even her choice of book was wilfully challenged.

Shuddering at the shame she felt at even writing that letter, Michelle looked out through the patio windows on to the immaculate garden, watching the wind anger the willow and the laurel and the tulips that remained. She loved that garden so much, the way it twisted and turned and went on forever, its nooks and crannies, the various hidey-holes with their sunshades and trailing roses and honeysuckle and strange artefacts bought for hundreds of pounds at reclamation yards. She wished it was hers and hers alone; of course she *owned* it, like she owned the house or part-owned it with Stephen, but she couldn't claim she *owned* its beauty – that was down to the gardener Alfie, because Stephen wasn't paying for expensive manicures only for her to get her hands dirty, and anyway he insisted that with their wealth it would be selfish not to provide work for the local gardener who'd dig for Britain for a minimum wage. The thought made her frown, and it was just then that she heard a familiar vibrating sound on the table. *It'll be one of the kids,* she thought, *they normally call on Saturday morning.* But when she picked up her phone she saw it was a mobile number she didn't recognise.

"Hello?" she said.

"Hi," he said, "it's Mark. The guy on the train."

"Oh God," she said.

"I just rang to say thank you for your letter, it really cheered me up."

"Wait a minute," she said, with a nervous glance at the door leading to the stairs before opening the door to the patio.

"If it's a bad time…" he said.

"No, really it's fine," she said, once outside.

"Anyway, yeah it really cheered me up. Especially your kind comments on *Cocoa Yard*."

"No, I genuinely did enjoy it," she said, "I was worried you'd think I was silly writing that letter, so many exclamation marks, and putting my number on the back."

"Not at all," he said with a chuckle, "it's very rare I get fanmail, believe it or not."

"Nonsense, I bet you're deluged."

"I wish. Anyway, I was worried too that you'd think *I* was silly putting my note in your book, or stalkerish even, especially as I'd put the earring in there too, the earring that wasn't even yours to return I now learn."

"It was very sweet of you," she said.

By the time they'd finished their conversation, Michelle found herself sitting under one of the sunshades near the bottom of the garden, the rich smell of honeysuckle squirting like perfume in the stiff breeze and the sound of sheep from the fields beyond. She'd no idea how long she was on the line for but she knew it was way past the time for Stephen's breakfast. Checking for signs of her husband in the bedroom window, she squirrelled her phone into her dressing-gown pocket and hurried back to the house. Closing the patio doors she realised her hands were shaking, so filling Stephen's cup seemed a trickier task than normal without splashing over the side. It was all so confusing, baffling even. She barely knew the man and there he was, calling on a Saturday morning, and there they were, talking as if they'd known each other for ages. They were laughing, saying silly things, agreeing they were like teenagers sending secret notes to each other across a classroom. Saying so much about themselves to each other, comparing notes on how life can be what it is, repetitive, dull, predictable, depressing. But the most baffling and unpredictable thing of all was that he'd asked if she'd like to meet up and she'd said yes.

"How far are you from Manchester?" he'd asked.

"Not too far," she'd lied, "Anyway, I can easily get a train or drive."

"It's just that I'm doing a signing Wednesday week. I wondered if you'd like to come along?"

And she'd said she would. Wednesday week, and they'd be in touch nearer the time to confirm.

When Michelle had taken a few minutes to compose herself, she took the tray up to the bedroom, cups rattling more than they normally would, and was surprised to see Stephen sitting up in bed, wide awake.

"Morning, Shell," he said, "I was just getting up."

"Sorry, it's a bit late."

"You were on that phone ages," he noted, not impatiently.

Michelle struggled not to betray her panic and said, "It was Jude. Calling to let me know she's back home."

"Ah," he said, "Thought it might be one of the kids."

"Not yet."

"Thanks," he said, when she put down his tray, "So how is she?"

"Who?"

"Jude, of course."

"Oh. Yeah she's… Yeah she's fine."

"Took a helluva long time to say she's fine. I mean I know you like sitting in your garden but you'd next to nothing on, you must've been freezing you poor thing."

"I didn't notice," she said, truthfully.

"Good job it isn't Alfie's day to do the gardens or he'd've had a nice surprise amid the floribundas! You flashing your chest."

She laughed at that, but sensed from his look that it wasn't entirely in jest, what he'd said.

"Is there something wrong?"

"Of course not."

"Are you sure? Is it about the Probins?"

"No, I've been looking at recipes actually."

"But there *is* something," he said, and she knew she'd have to give him something.

"OK," she said, struggling to swallow and fearing the truth would come tumbling out, "it's about London."

"What about London?"

"We had a row. Me and Jude."

"What about?"

"Oh things, you know."

"What things?"

"Oh she said something about what I was wearing, you know what women are like, we take it personally. Stephen, do you think I'm old-fashioned?"

"Old-fashioned?"

"The way I dress."

"Not really," he said.

"So you do."

"I didn't say that!" he said, "Is everything OK, Shell?"

"Yea I'm fine," she said, "So anyway that was us having it out just now. Jude apologising and me fessing up to being over-sensitive. We're fine now, I feel much happier."

"Good," said Stephen as she turned to leave the room, "Because don't go, I've got something else that'll cheer you up. I've been keeping something secret. I was going to wait till tonight at the dinner party but had second thoughts 'cause it'd seem show-offy in front of the Probins."

"What would? What secret?"

"We're going to New York."

"New York!"

"I've been, you haven't, but you've always wanted to. I've booked some time off, I can show you the sights. Thing is, Shell, I've come to a realisation."

"What realisation?"

"You're bored."

Michelle couldn't control the flicker of guilt she knew had crossed her face. Why was he saying this? Had he heard some of her conversation with Mark? The shaky hands returned and she wrang them, trying to strangle their betrayal.

"I work too much," he went on, "which means I don't pay you enough attention. So I made a decision. I told Ian I was having a fortnight's holiday and I wasn't taking no for an answer, and I was taking you to America, to which I'm also not taking no for an answer. And this afternoon you and me are going shopping to get you some new attire!"

"I can't believe it," she said, masking her discomfiture.

"Believe it," he said firmly, "Believe that soon you'll be in Manhattan and all its wonders, sitting in the biggest garden there is, Central Park! And what's more, you can catch up with Jude and she can say sorry for whatever she said to you face to face. And you'll be dressed in the best stuff money can buy and you'll show her who's old-fashioned."

"I'll phone and tell her," Michelle said, still struggling to make sense of all this, "When are you thinking?"

"Next Friday, for two weeks."

Next Friday? But that would mean…

"I can see you're flabbergasted," he said, "You don't have to say anything."

"I'm sorry I'm just so shocked. That's wonderful," she said with heroic effort, before turning to leave the room, doubtless to bang her fists down on the kitchen table in frustration.

"Don't go," he said again, patting the space in the bed beside him, the space she left but tossed and turned in last night, "Get in."

"But we have to go shopping," she said, "Not just for clothes, I need ingredients for tonight's dinner."

"Later," Stephen said, "Take off the dressing gown, show me that beautiful body of yours and get in."

With confusion swilling around her head, Michelle knew there was no point arguing. She would take off her dressing-gown, get in beside him and do her best to please. But this time she'd know it wasn't just because it was expected, because she didn't want to lose his friendship or because she loved him for that and not for anything else. This time she'd be doing it because she knew that if she refused, it would be because she would rather be getting into bed with *someone* else.

*

Him.

Mark loved his Saturday mornings, spent largely reading the Guardian with his feet up. First he'd scan the sports pages, then the news, saving his favourite part, the cryptic crossword, till last. He relished trying to crack the code, vying with the compiler for supremacy, feeling great when he'd managed to get inside their mind. Every Saturday morning was like this, basking in the sheer bliss of peace and solitude because Carol was at pilates. While it was agreed that the morning was there for his selfish delectation, it was also agreed that he'd prepare the lunch or take her somewhere nice in town. With money tight it had lately been the former, so today he was pitting his wits against the crossword setter while a casserole was bubbling not without merriment in the kitchen. By the time he'd completed the grid and meticulously gone over the pencil with pen, cut it out and put it in an envelope for submission, the casserole was ready and Carol's Mini heard in the drive.

"How was pilates?" he said, meeting her in the kitchen.

"Oh you know," she said.

As a matter of fact he didn't know, but he omitted to say so.

"It was OK. Katy got on my tits though."

"Really?" he said, as committed as possible.

"Banging on about her kids as usual. Honestly you'd think she was the only woman alive to have given birth to a sprog."

"I'm surprised you have time to talk about anything if you're busy jumping up and down or whatever," he said.

"No! This was in the car on the way home. Bored me rigid, I had to switch on the radio. David Bowie came on and she wittered all the way through him."

"I made a casserole," he said, by way of compensation.

"Lovely. And I bought some wine because I need it and have the right to drink it now I've had a workout. How was your morning?"

"Oh you know," he said, with barely concealed irony.

"Did you finish the crossword?"

"In record time."

"I'll take a quick shower while you serve up."

As Carol raced up the stairs, Mark began to dish out the food. He stole a sip from the ladel and was pleased at the taste, priding himself on another job well done. He was in good spirits. It had been a good Saturday morning in which he'd done nothing unusual apart from one thing, phoning Michelle and arranging to meet up. Of course he knew it was foolish in a way, childish even, they'd said so on the phone and laughed about it, yet it was something filling him with strange emotions, not least of which excitement, the thing he'd realised he'd been craving all this time. Days spent trying to write and failing or producing some ridiculous doggerel or angry tirade against Brexit, dreading Carol coming home from school, masturbating perfunctorily, swearing at Derek shitting on the lawn and losing his temper with the blasted cable of the mower and how it never quite fit where he wanted it to fit in the shed with the spiders. Now these days till Wednesday week would be all of that, plus something else, the anticipation of seeing her beautiful face again. And what, if he were honest, was so childish about that? But there was also one even more significant thing about this day in particular, this Saturday that was partly there for his delectation and partly there for Carol's pilates – this was the day he'd be telling her he wanted them to break up.

*

Her too.

Carol loved a cool shower after pilates, she loved its gentle pressure turning her reddened skin back to its normal white, and she loved most the way these Saturdays kept her in shape, made her still look good. She knew that Pete Threadgold fancied her; he'd never said as much but did once drop the less than subtle hint that he liked redheads. She knew that when she left the staff room in her tight dress, he admired her ass and he was not the only one, not the only one to fancy what they knew they couldn't have because she'd got Mark.

She'd said nothing more about the letter from the girl who pretentiously called herself the sleeper on the train, and the phone number on the back, and her jealousy that Mark had slipped a note into the book he wrote that she was reading. She hadn't felt the need, because Mark was a good man whose intention wasn't flirtatious, it was genuinely innocent, and typical of the man who didn't seek fame, who would've been so embarrassed and too self-effacing to tell the girl he was the author. She deeply regretted telling him his work was shit that day. He wasn't shit. He was Mark, the man she loved, and would finish her shower and fuck the way they used to fuck with all the lusty verve of the teenagers in Miami.

*

Her.

When Stephen had finished what he wanted to do, Michelle let him cradle her.

"That was nice," he said.

"Good," she said.

"I'm not going to ask how was it for you," he joked, and she laughed. He did so love his pillow-talk.

"I do love you, Stephen," she said.

"And I love you," he said, and there was a long pause where she could hear his heart beating like a drum roll, before he added, "It wasn't Jude on the phone, was it?"

Michelle could feel the blood drain out of her, as if someone had hung her on a wall and cut off her feet.

"Don't worry," he said, "I don't want you to say anything. I just know all this isn't enough. The house, the car… It's not things you need, it's excitement. And it would break my heart if you got it from someone else."

*

Him.

It had been a blazing row, and Mark was sitting alone in the house to come to terms with it, play it over and over in his mind. Carol had slammed out and gone to her mother's or Katy's or some other friend's, he didn't know. He did care, but didn't know. He didn't like hurting her. Ridiculous she said it was, this infatuation with a woman who happened to be reading his book. Vainglorious, to have his head turned like this, and to sacrifice what he has for five minutes of fame and gratification, and by the way she suspected he'd masturbated over her, wasn't that what he did almost every day with the time while not writing some shit or other? She had suitors too, she said, no shortage of offers down the years, talk of the staff room she was, they commented on her ass when she wore her tight dress, and now she wishes she'd succumbed to the advances she'd often had, not just from the likes of Pete fucking Threadgold. Perhaps things would've been different, he thought, if they *had* got married all those years ago when they drunkenly proposed to each other and she bought him flowers? Or if he was still successful. Things had gone stale. A poxy signing in Manchester Wednesday week, where he'd shift a couple of copies of *Cocoa Yard*. So what? Or if he didn't have to keep walking the fucking dog and taking Fluoxetine that didn't make a scrap of difference. Or if he was man enough to just accept what he had and enjoy it. Perhaps Carol was right, there *was* an element of self-gratification here. He hated himself now, but at the same time he maintained that youthful excitement and avid anticipation of seeing Michelle again on Wednesday week.

In slamming out of their house, making the curtains plume and the ornaments rattle on their shelf, Carol had left her wine and he eyed it, pondering the ethics of toasting this occasion, monumental as it was, with the wine purchased with her hard-earned cash. But then he said to himself, *What did it matter?* He'd hurt the woman and it was impossible to unhurt her. While a person is unique, irreplaceable, this was just a bottle of plonk.

And so there he was, sipping it, thinking of the future, when suddenly his phone bleeped with a text:

I'm so sorry I can't do Wednesday week. I don't think this is such a good idea after all. Please forgive me, M.

*

Her.

Having sent the text, blocked the number and carefully placed the novel in the recycle bin along with its note inside the pages, Michelle returned to the kitchen and the internet recipes for dinner with the Probins. Stephen was upstairs showering and getting ready for their afternoon of shopping, which she knew would be lovely. They'd laugh, hold hands, and he'd urge her to try things on she liked the look of and she would say it's too expensive and he'd say so what, she'd look nice in it, even Jude would be jealous. She loved that man, and now realised how stupid she'd been since that day when a man on a train who happened to be the author of the book she was reading showed kindness towards her and gave her some attention. No, she decided, that's all it was and all it would ever be, a brief look into something new. And later when they came home from town she'd cook something delicious for the Probins, and over dinner she'd laugh and talk, doing her best to enjoy the occasion, and she'd do it not just for her husband but do it for herself as well.

*

Her too.

In a layby some miles away, Carol opened the encyclopaedia and found between the words Florida and flower, the biscuited token of many heartbeats ago. Sickened with rage, she opened her window and crumbled it to dust.

*

Him.

In the kitchen, Mark opened the second bottle and gazed out onto the garden, where Derek was doing what he came to do. He frowned but didn't really care. He knew it was foolish to expect the woman he didn't even know to come and meet him. Carol was right, it was ridiculous to suppose that could happen. He'd said only a few words to her before she went to sleep, and right now he deeply regretted slipping the note and the earring into the book she was reading which happened to be the one he'd penned. Of course she was married, he remembered when admiring her finger nails manicured and painted like pearls that one of them was wearing a ring. Right now, he imagined, she was deleting his number and preparing to delete him from her life and turn back to the man she loved, spend the day with him and sleep with him tonight.

With that final blocked image in his mind, Mark poured from the second bottle and took it to the sitting room, fully intent on getting drunk, then retiring to bed alone.

Them.
Shit. Nothing happened.

"Bedfellows"

"Are you sure you don't want to come old man?" Bill asked.

George didn't reply. He'd been off-colour for about a week and Bill said as much. "You've been off-colour for about a week," he said.

Again George didn't respond, he just slouched in his chair with the energy only to feel sorry for himself.

"Well, I'll bring something back for that cough old man," said Bill, and with a heavy heart he shut the door at the stern and jumped deftly for his age down to the towpath, swinging his satchel over his shoulder.

They'd moored at this spot before, many times and always this time of year, and Bill was surprised or not so surprised to see how much it had altered in just twelve months; the fields now clustered with Caramac-coloured houses, some of them with double garages—almost like garages with houses attached rather than the other way about, he mused. Swan Drive, Mallard Way, Heron Crescent and Otter Close, the unadopted and not yet tarmacked new streets he combed through on his way to town all named after the birds and animals that had been displaced by human beings needing housed. *A pity*, he thought, *but then again don't most people need a street to live on?*

Bill and George, however, were not most people; they had lived on a narrowboat for fourteen years, enjoying peace and tranquillity in their dotage, living simply and frugally, sometimes off the lands they meandered. Fourteen years of luxurious off-grid life, the window of which looked out on a different garden every single day. Of course it wasn't possible to live entirely without money so Bill tried to make some small amounts from his paintings and sketches, mostly of birds and animals or the scenery he observed, but sometimes of passers-by or their children or their pets, mostly but not exclusively dogs. If Bill and George had enough food for the two of them and the birds Bill liked to feed wherever they moored, they were quite content with that. On days weather permitting he'd set up his easel on the towpath, hoping to catch the eye of ramblers. George couldn't paint, so he'd just sit napping with a tin in front of him lest anyone was inclined to drop in a coin or two. Yesterday they'd had a good day; Bill had been 'commissioned' to compose a cartoon sketch of a group from the Shropshire Ramblers Association, for which he charged £50. Privately the ramblers were amused at this odd couple, dishevelled as they were, and the clubbed-together commission was more out of pity than of charity, though that was a detail Bill and George were blissfully oblivious to.

This had been their life since 2004 when Bill lost his job in the library. At the age of fifty-seven he struggled to adapt to not working and when he'd been unlucky with numerous job applications, he became rather depressed. But just as he was at his wits' end, exacerbated by the fact his severance was quickly being eaten away, he had an epiphany. Something of a loner, he'd often contemplated living off-grid in either a caravan or a barge. So the day of his revelation he did some digging and found a boat for sale in a marina near Barbridge on the Shropshire Union Canal. It was called Bill, and seeing this as a significant livery, eponymous Bill paid the asking price of £70,000 o.n.o. With the rest and almost very last of his money, he did up the boat, replaced some of the rotten underboards and painted the hull. Then come day of the launch, when he'd closed his bank account, handed the key in to his landlord and binned his mobile phone, he turned his back on *that* life and all its trappings and headed for a new one devoid of cruelty or controversy or malice.

That was also the day he met George. They immediately hit it off and both knew that after spending increasing amounts of time knocking about together they would ultimately share this new home, and share it they have for fourteen years. Over time the bond between the two was reinforced, never a bad word spoken, never a disagreeable exchange, always the best of friends with the fortitude that only complete trust and gradual love can provide, sharing a bed and welcoming the comfort and warmth from each other's bodies especially on those chilly nights when the log burner clicked its embers. It was and still is the perfect relationship. Bill had intended to change the livery and add George's name but never quite got round to it, but anyway it wasn't an issue and George could never have requested it. In George's eyes, the boat belonged to *them*, it was their home and that was all there was to it. A tacit agreement that they'd rub along like this till either or both popped their clogs.

While most of their life was desultory, unhurried and free, structure was occasionally determined by some sort of event, this week being an example of that, where they'd slowly carved the waters through Shropshire into Cheshire, arriving at the small agricultural town called Nantwich and its Food Festival, a particular draw for the two of them and vital source of sustenance. And so this is why Bill was leaving his sick friend behind to go and buy food and medicine, intending to fork out as little as possible of the £50 in his leather purse.

As he approached the town, he could hear the thud of live music and see the many drawn towards it, dressed minimally in the afternoon heatwave. He crossed Waterlode and headed into the car park which had been requisitioned for the festival, a jumbled kaleidoscope of tents, marquees and stalls. There were touts handing out flyers, laughing adults standing in groups to drink beer, eat pizza and burgers, and children licking melted ice cream that dribbled down their cones and arms. The sight and smell of all this made Bill feel hungry – he and George hadn't eaten since breakfast, though George hadn't managed much at all before sicking it overboard.

Bill knitted his way through the slow-moving or static throng and headed for Swinemarket which he remembered had a Boots. Along the way, he stopped momentarily at various stalls, sampling dice of cheese, cake, flapjack and biscuits, intending to fill his belly for free. He thought about George and wondered if he was now hungry – he'd make sure he'd get back to the boat with his satchel full of fruit, veg and meat. Tonight they'd eat like kings, and if he could get something for George's cough all the better. They'd even have a glass of beer if he could find some stall selling it cheap. Bill was a connoisseur of real ale, and often thought of brewing his own but this was another thing he never quite got round to, and anyway the boat lacked space for extra vessels in which to keep it.

By the time Bill had filled his gut and his satchel, his boots rubbed and he was tired of drifting along in the slow ebb of foodies. It was hot and he was thirsty, so he opened one of the beers and sat for a while on the grass by St Mary's Church to enjoy its quenching bitterness while watching the many people saunter by or lounge in the shade of walnut trees, and the children dancing to the music – he would paint this scene tomorrow, he decided, when George would be fit enough to sit with his tin in front of him lest anyone was inclined to drop in a coin or two.

As the bottle was gradually emptied, Bill continued to watch the children and lost himself in his thoughts. He thought about the years he worked in the library, seen as the local font of everything knowledge, a misfit, a loner who only spoke when to a reader seeking a copy of something or other, or needing direction to some department or other. Once his working day had finished he'd lock the doors and walk the three miles past the primary school to his home where he lived alone with his paintings and books. His evenings once he'd cooked and eaten a simple repast were spent water colouring or reading or listening to the radio. He prided himself on never missing a single episode of *Just a Minute*. He had never owned a television. He had no family besides a brother somewhere or other, to whom he hadn't spoken and from whom he hadn't heard in years. He had no friends and he was happy with that, glad to be alone, inspired by his private view of the world and vivid imagination to paint. That was his life until what that wicked little girl Masie Donahoe said about him changed everything.

Shuddering out of this reverie, Bill thought of George and began to feel guilty about leaving him alone so long. What if his health had worsened? What if he'd been sick again? What if he'd died? Concerned, Bill slaked the last of his thirst, discarded the empty bottle and rejoined the drifting hordes until washed up on Waterlode then Welsh Row, where he headed up the sparser paths towards the cut.

By the time he reached the towpath and saw in the distance their beloved home, Bill's feet and brow were sweating and blistered and he was glad and relieved to see the wisps of smoke coil from the boat's chimney. He could hear the low sound of the generator, churning like a nightjar. There was no sign of George, whom he hoped would've rested by now and be fit enough for an evening meal; boiled potatoes, cabbage, carrots and a nice piece of steak he'd fetched from the market and which he hoped George could now stomach.

"George," he called, with a knock on the stern door, "I fetched something for that cough old man."

But there was no cough. There was no response at all. Worried, Bill opened the door and ventured down the steps inside. The hours were now fading and it was that stage in the evening when if they didn't have the lights on, the boat could feel rather chilly and unwelcoming, especially when the logs were burning grey and dusty towards their death. He had a bad feeling, a horrible vision of George cold in his chair, eyes closed having drawn his last breath. There'd be nobody to inform, George had nobody except him, but there'd be a 'funeral' to organise, some sort of fitting send-off and celebration of a long life and of a long friendship without question or agenda, devoid of cruelty or malice, trappings or controversy. But just as Bill was thinking the awful thought of any procedure if his friend were gone, George finally broke the silence and came up to greet him, lick his legs, wag his tail and sniff hungrily at the satchel his friend and master dropped to the floor.

*

"Mr Johnson's Dragon"

"Which house did you say?" said Mr Johnson.

"Kestrel," said Neil.

"Ah, Kestrel. It always struck me as amusing to name them after birds. I never said as much to the Headmaster of course."

"You taught me for five years," said Neil, trying not to sound annoyed at being unremembered still.

"Such a long time ago, you see," said Mr Johnson, "And I'm afraid my faculties, they er…"

They were in the kitchen of Mr Johnson's large Georgian house in Didsbury, drinking tea from the pot he'd freshly brewed, from bone china cups belonging to a service he explained was missing two cups and three saucers due to breakage. And if Mrs Johnson were still alive she'd be vexed with him for being so clumsy.

Neil had been back in Didsbury for two months having spent the previous forty years elsewhere. He'd taken a flat near to where Mr Johnson lived, but in the not-so-leafy and sought-after part because it was all he could afford. The six-month tenancy he'd signed would be enough, he'd decided, before moving on again, because that was his way. He was a freelance journalist and he always felt the necessity to go and look for story rather than wait for it to come to him, or at any rate that was his philosophy, and anyway journo or no journo he enjoyed travel, seeing new places, meeting people, some of them new some of them old…

They'd bumped into each other in the high street that morning, or, to be more accurate, Neil had bumped into Mr Johnson.

"I'm terribly sorry," he said.

"That's quite all right, young man," said the old man.

"Sir!" exclaimed Neil, "It's you!"

"I'm sorry I…"

"Mr Johnson! Grammar School! Woodwork!"

"Ah, yes indeed, bang to rights. I taught there for many years. But I…"

"Sorry, sir, Neil Welsh."

"Neil Walsh, er…"

"Welsh."

"Ah Welsh let me see. Neil you say?"

"Yes, sir."

"Oh now come, come," said Mr Johnson with a touch of irritation, "I'm sure there's no requirement for formalities after all this erm…"

"Forty years," said Neil.

"Forty years. Well now. Is it really?"

And they'd talked a little while on the pavement outside Costa, Neil explaining he was a journalist and back in the area, and Mr Johnson seeming not a jot impressed and joking that he can't have been a very inspiring teacher if he hadn't considered carpentry as a profession, and recalling with sadness that he'd been retired for over thirty years and didn't get out much as he was only able to walk with the aid of a stick; he'd thought about one of those mobility thingummyjigs but reckoned he'd be a hazard to children. And they'd laughed at that, causing Mr Johnson to wobble slightly and Neil having to steady him. Mr Johnson had said he was right as ninepence but Neil had insisted he walk him to his house to make sure he got home safely, and if it was just around the corner it was absolutely no trouble, he wasn't in any kind of hurry. He didn't correct Mr Johnson when he suggested carpentry hadn't been something to consider as a profession.

"Now for that cup of tea," he said to Neil when he'd helped him through the hall and into the kitchen at the far end of the house, "By way of remuneration for your kindness."

"No need to think of it like that," said Neil, "You're very welcome. You nearly came quite a cropper out there."

"And not for the first time!" laughed Mr Johnson, filling the kettle, "I was a fool to venture out, bound to be busy on what I believe they call Black Friday. All nonsense in my view calling a Friday or any day for that matter black." His hands were unsteady, causing some of the water to splash on his clothes though he seemed not to notice.

It was a large gloomy kitchen which Neil could see led off to other smaller gloomier rooms, perhaps a laundry room and downstairs toilet. He knew lots of houses like this, many of which now converted into flats, and was somehow reassured that this was one of the survivors, yet somehow would have to admit if challenged that it was a waste as it probably had six bedrooms that could house six persons instead of just a single elderly one. It depended how you looked at it, he supposed, as he watched the old man swill boiling water around the teapot before tipping it out then putting in two spoonfuls of tea and refilling it.

"Now we'll allow that to brew," he said, "while we take the weight off our feet."

"I feel guilty," said Neil, "I should've offered to make it."

"Nonsense!" said Mr Johnson, "Now, which house did you say?"

"Kestrel."

"Neil Walsh, Kestrel."

"Welsh."

"Neil Welsh. You didn't perhaps have an older brother?"

"No," said Neil, "I'm an only child."

"And were you particularly bright? It would worry me if you were particularly bright you see, because I always remember the particularly bright ones."

"Really," muttered Neil.

"Pardon?"

"I said neither particularly bright nor utterly dim."

"Ah," said Mr Johnson, rising crookedly from his chair to pour the tea.

"I suppose I was average really."

"Do help yourself to milk and sugar, as much as you need of course."

"Thank you," said Neil, "Anyway, it doesn't matter."

"What doesn't?"

"That you can't remember me, it doesn't matter."

"So many pupils, or students I believe they call you now, come and go you see. So many faces, so many names. You're not the first to stop me in the street or in a shop and say, 'Hello Mr Johnson!' and I say, 'Hello!' and can't quite put my finger on it."

"Perhaps they don't all bump into you and nearly send you flying," laughed Neil.

"That's true, er…" Mr Johnson said, looking at him over the rim of his cup, his shaking hand causing it to wobble and spill into the saucer then down his front like a miniature fountain. He had beady eyes still, but nowadays magnified by very thick spectacles, and his hair that was always cropped was balding and grown long at the back, probably fixed in place with Brylcreem or something or other. Back then, Neil only ever saw him in a white overall so it was difficult to tell if he was tidy or unkempt, but easy now to see it was the latter – his grey trousers were shiny from many years' friction and he'd detected a slight evidence of cack at the rear when he was at the stove. His shirt had a dirty neck and his tie hadn't been tucked under the collar on one side. The cardigan that covered it was badged with various dinners.

"Sadly I don't seem to bother much these days," he said, as if reading Neil's mind, "With anything. People for instance. I don't socialise you see, most of my friends and colleagues are dead. I don't know if you recall Eddie Latham, Mr Latham to you?"

"Science."

"The last of the gang to die. They buried him four years ago, I think. I went to his funeral, packed to the rafters it was! Oh there were many alumni in attendance, a popular man, a fine man and a fine teacher. I thought, *It'll be you next, Johnson*. Sometimes I'm surprised to wake up in the morning. Sometimes I say to myself, "Oh God not again!" Some days go by and I speak to nobody but myself. Nobody but myself… Yes I'm afraid you get out of the habit of talking when you get to this age. Not much chance of the chapel being packed to the rafters when *I* pop me clogs! Ha."

"That is sad," said Neil, and might have added, "but true."

Though Neil was irked not to be remembered, he was not in the slightest surprised. Looking at the frail old thing that sat across the table from him, you wouldn't believe he used to be a giant and tyrant of a man, feared by all the pupils and, Neil shouldn't wonder, by the staff too. In fact, if Johnson had told the Head he found the idea of naming forms after birds amusing, it's conceivable that the Head would've taken flight in terror. It was no surprise at all to Neil that he lived alone and had no friends. He wondered even if Mr Latham was actually his friend. And it would be no shock at all if Johnson were cremated with not a single soul in the chapel to sit in black and mumble *Crimond*.

"How long ago did Mrs Johnson die?" he asked, after a lengthy pause, "If you don't mind my asking?"

"Not at all," he said, "Let me see, must be ten years. Ah she was ready to go in the end. Nasty business it was. Nasty, nasty business."

"Nasty?"

"Poor girl went batty. Oh they said I could put her in a home of course. I didn't think that was right, you understand. We said till death do us part and we meant it! She wasn't going into a home, not as long as I was still breathing!" Johnson banged the table at that, causing the spoons to dance, then needed a drink of tea to wet his mouth where spittle caked in the corners.

"So what happened?"

"Poor girl fell. That's what did for her in the end, not the fact that she'd lost her faculties."

"I'm sorry to hear that."

"Lost her footing on them stairs she did."

Neil looked behind him down the corridor to the hall, where the newel post acted as Johnson's coat-hanger, and imagined the poor old girl going cold, broken-necked at the foot of the stairs, then looked back at Johnson and saw he was crying.

"I'm very sorry, sir," he said, "I didn't mean to bring it all up."

"I was out at the time, at the chemist, fetching her prescription. Came home and found her there. To this day I wish I'd been quicker, then perhaps…"

"I'm very sorry, sir," Neil repeated again.

"Tragic," Johnson spat as if spitting out the awful memory, "And I thought we'd agreed you would refrain from calling me sir!"

"It's just I remember her too," said Neil, "English right?"

"And a very fine teacher she was. Respected."

"She had a temper if you don't mind my saying so."

"Ha. The dragon I would call her. Affectionately only you understand, and in the privacy of our home not in work. She *did* have a temper, like me I suppose. But I respected her," he said proudly, "Like she respected me. I was deeply impressed with her knowledge of Shakespeare, she could recite long, long passages from most if not all of his works, plays, sonnets alike. *Whether 'tis nobler in the mind to take arms against a sea of troubles and by opposing end them?* And she was deeply impressed with my carpentry skills you know."

"I'm sure."

"Oh yes," Johnson said, rising to replenish their cups, "she was a great fan of my carvings in particular, one of which gave her immense pleasure. Pride of place on the bedroom wall for years and still is. I used to say it was a bugger to dust, so intricate were its markings so minute was the detail in places, working the grain with chisels large and needle-thin. But she wouldn't let me take it down you see, I wouldn't have her lose her temper over that!"

It's true they both had a temper, Neil remembered all too well. But he, Mr Johnson, could also be unfair and cruel. During exams in his fourth year, Johnson was the adjudicator sitting at the front of Kestrel, where Neil was poring over his 'O' Level history paper. When handed in, the pupils were supposed to wait while the adjudicator gathered in the papers and made sure they were all present and alphabetical. But Johnson went further and began to read, and suddenly laughed sarcastically. As the pupils fidgeted and exchanged nervous glances, wondering whose paper caused such mirth, Johnson sensed the current, looked Neil in the eye and said, "Yes, it's yours, lad, and don't expect me not to pour scorn on it. I am not in the habit of celebrating mediocrity or woeful lack of knowledge." Neil could only look at his neighbour and best friend, David Turner, and shrug, but inside he was maddened and humiliated, and privately afterwards he'd wept in the toilets. Then came the time when he handed in his piece for woodwork, on which over the weeks and months he'd toiled with great care and, he thought, dexterity and artistry. But when Johnson received his piece he dismissed it to the floor and said, "Not what was asked for, lad! It's a waste of good timber. I hardly think it's going to be carpentry for you! You will only ever be average in whatever you amount to, if you amount to anything at all!" But Johnson was wrong, it was a brilliant carving he'd summoned from the depths of his imagination having been read mythical stories by his father at bedtime. Pratchett, Tolkien, and yarns his father had concocted himself of weird characters and monsters, hobbits, dragons and the phoenix. The carving he handed in was to him, and incidentally to David and the rest of his classmates, evocative, beautiful and worthy of any wall. And carpentry happened to be the thing Neil most loved, and most wanted to consider as a profession. Weeks later, when it came to collecting the work and taking it home to show his parents, Johnson told him it was no longer in the store cupboard, he'd thrown it away. In those days, there was no recourse to complain; the Grammar School system was like that, punishments were given and taken, blows were dealt and suffered with silent smarting, cruelty taken as read. It didn't matter if you were particularly bright or average or poor, cruelty was allowed and encouraged to breed on a level playing field. And actually Neil *was* particularly bright, memorably so, and forty years on he often reflected on that, harbouring the resentment at the humiliation, the fact that if his teachers had been better, he may have fared better too, that it wasn't his innate ability that was in question, more the boredom and disinterest felt in uninspiring lessons led by uninspiring teachers.

After tea, Neil decided to ride the bus back, the weight of the thing in his bag not inconsiderable. But he walked to the bus stop with purpose, the surety of his gait contrasting with the uncertainty in his mind. Was this actually the carving? It didn't matter that he'd engineered bumping into Johnson in the street, or that he'd insisted quite forcefully on escorting the man home after his near fall. And it made no odds that he'd said he was very thirsty on the doorstep of Johnson's home, and lied he was diabetic and needed the sugar and a sweet cup of tea was essential or there'd be another incident and this time an ambulance would be necessary. He felt a twinge of guilt at the look of anguish in the man's eyes when he said what he said about that time all those years ago, and the sweat on the man's brow. But like that man, Neil would shrug off the memory of a nasty, nasty business. The humiliation and shame, the dullness of lessons, the cruelty, the uncorroborated or unreported stories of what happened in the store room, the dubiousness of Johnson's version of events to the police surrounding the dragon's death. Like Johnson, he would shrug off the memory of being caught in the man's bedroom having gone upstairs on the pretext of needing the toilet, the claim and counter-claim, the deal he tried to broker at the top of the stairs that meant if he got what was his he'd make no historical allegations, the brief struggle that followed before his departure from the house. Yes, he was not to be feeling too bad about what he'd done, because he'd done it for a reason.

So when he found his seat on the bus, he took the carving from his bag. He ran his fingers over it, recognising and enjoying its cold curves, its contours, the way the grain worked and he'd worked with the grain. "A lovely piece of timber, Welsh," Johnson had said, "Teak. An expensive piece, lad, so don't waste it." And he hadn't wasted it, he'd made it work, he'd created a thing of beauty inspired by his father and the stories he read to him at bedtime, the thing he was enjoying

71

right now, that was worthy of any wall and that he'd been denied the opportunity to *show it* to his father before he passed away. And when he turned it over, there on the back, and faintly but indelibly, were the final marks of the chisel – the letters *N W*.

"That's nice," said a lady on the seat opposite, "Who made it?"

"A fifteen-year-old boy called Neil Welsh who would probably not amount to much," he proudly said, and clutched the thing to his chest.

*

"The Birds Are Dead"

He was seven years old, a latch-key kid in half-mast trousers the day he went to hell. He'd been to school and got into trouble, hauled out of assembly for adapting the Lord's Prayer – Our Father who farts in heaven – and Mr McDonald had him by the scruff of the neck and half-dragged half-carried him back to the classroom where he was made to face the wall the rest of the day and go without his dinner, and even when he asked to use the toilet, he was refused so shat his pants. In that undignified and unwitting protest, he stole his chance during afternoon break and walked with small steps out of the classroom and out of the school altogether. His mum was at work and father was absent, ran out on them the year before so that was OK, he'd join the older kids who truanted.

So he wheeled his bike from the shed and rode it, pants full of drying waste, to Peacock Farm. On the way he saw Julie Parry coming back and she stopped, using her shoes as brakes. "The birds are dead," she said.

At Peacock Farm there was a barn they made a den of, and Gilbert and the others, some eight years older than the boy, caught two baby sparrows, put them in a wooden box and overnight underneath lit a candle designed to keep them warm. But starved of food they perished and it was up to Julie to eulogise in her scuffed brogues.

When he got there, most of the boys had gone, only Gilbert remained, and the two of them scooped up the baby birds one each and performed a burial then lit cigarettes the older one had stolen from the village shop.

"What's that stink?" he said as they sat to smoke, "Have you shit yourself?"

"No," the boy lied.

"You have, you dirty little bastard," Gilbert said, grabbing his throat and adding that people who shit themselves are destined for hell and no wonder his dad ran out on them. Reminded horribly of what Mr McDonald had said about those who take the Lord's name in vain, the boy was now convinced it was true – he *was* going to hell. That night if he slept, he'd wake up dead like the birds. He couldn't go home. So when it was dusk and even Gilbert had pedalled off, he remained in the barn, eyes wide open, refusing to go to sleep, listening to the peacocks that were living there cry.

At home, the mother had returned from work to find it empty; the latch-key kid nowhere to be seen. At first, she reflected this was normal enough, the boy would often go roaming and come back with empty belly, but as time ticked on she got worried then desperate then definite that terrible things were happening to her boy, the distant peacocks' cries were his. Then there was a visit from Mr McDonald who told her the boy had been in trouble for blasphemy and had walked out of school uninvited, and that was the nail in his coffin as far as she could see. With profuse apologies to the teacher on her son's behalf, she deftly employed the neighbours to go in search, heading automatically and hopefully for the cries of the peacocks.

Back in the barn the boy sat, smelling himself, shifting uncomfortably as the turd in his pants had hardened and grown sharp, fighting the sleep he now needed. For hours seeming like days, until he heard voices and spied through a crack in the wood some shards of light from torches. And that was how he was found.

Safely delivered to his mother, he cried into her breast, saying he was sorry he killed the birds and took the Lord's name in vain and made his dad go missing, but he cacked his pants because Mr McDonald wouldn't excuse him so couldn't come home.

When all was said and done, the woman was glad to have her latch-key kid back in her arms and cleaned him up and let him sleep with her that night, to reassure him it wasn't his fault there was a space in her bed, as far as she was concerned his father was the one who'd died and if he was anywhere at all it surely wouldn't be heaven. If anyone was going to hell it was that man, or Mr McDonald, and tomorrow the latch-key kid would go to school accompanied by a note saying stiffly that if in future her kid wanted to use the lavatory, he should be granted permission, no ifs or buts, Lord's Prayer or no Lord's Prayer.

And thus the kid finally slept, safe in the knowledge that while there'd be no tomorrow for the sparrows or his father, there would be one for him. A tomorrow on which he would walk as tall as storeys.

*

"Four and Twenty Blackbirds"

In a windowless florescent-bright room, she was young and beautiful whereas he wasn't. In fact she was thirty years young and he was fifty, or more, years old. Why though, did he feel she was looking at him in *that* way? Because that was his wont. He was supposed to be looking not for sex but for talent to augment the department he headed in his opinion quite immaculately and on an impressively upwards professional spiral. Sex, if any at such functions, would be a bonus. It was a business conference over two days, designed to launch new products and to be informal, fun, inspiring, and all of the above boxes were being ticked. Not that he was a man fond of ticking boxes, or in fact that very phrase. He was not modern in his approach, nor was he old-school, he was just plain excellent, as excellent as the contribution the young woman was making to the morning's session. So much so that he would have to compliment her during lunch for standing out amid the throng of forty.

"I really want to work for this company," she said, over a plate of chips and nothing else because, she declared, she needed the carbs. "It's been my ambition to work for this company for so many years. I've followed your career, read your papers, attended your lectures, and always been inspired."

"How many years exactly?" he asked, impressed.

"Ten. Or more," she confirmed, "To be honest I can't be exact. Would that matter?"

"No," he assured, "I'd rather you be honest than exact."

She smiled and he smiled back and something strange happened. Strange, surprising and certainly unexpected. She reached over her plate and touched his hand and said, "I really like how you dress by the way."

"The way I dress?"

"It's cool."

For some reason he expected another line, a qualification or disclaimer, something like "…for a man of your age." But this was neither in the offing nor apparently in her mind. The compliment was honest and genuine, so much so that he now knew with absolute certainty that later that night, they might possibly be sleeping together maybe…

*

"I couldn't concentrate this afternoon," he said, as they sipped wine over dinner in the hotel his employers had booked for him and paid for.

"Why not?"

"Because I was thinking about what you said. About the way I dress, and it being cool."

"I meant it."

"Thanks. It's true I make the effort."

"Hope it didn't weird you out?"

He was aware of, but had never used, that phrase and went with it. "Not at all. When you said that over lunch I took it to be very genuine and not designed to curry favour-"

"I never have curry with chips."

He laughed at that, and so did she, as she went on… "So you want us to be honest?"

"Of course."

"I agree your performance wasn't brilliant this afternoon, if I'm *absolutely* honest. Your delivery kind of lacked focus."

"I was distracted. Which rarely happens."

"It was me, wasn't it? You were thinking about how I looked naked and I was thinking the same about you. You knew I was making a worthy contribution to the session and I knew that too, like I knew you were impressed. And I know I'll be good for the company and you know that too. You knew we'd be sleeping together tonight and so did I."

It was a long speech that rendered him speechless. Not because he was uncomfortable with what she was saying, quite the opposite, but because it was so sudden, so forthright, so confident and surprising given his rank and hers and his age and hers.

"It doesn't bother me," she said, before another sip and apparently reading his mind through refraction in her glass. "How old you are."

"Good," he said.

"So I'll go on."

"With what?"

"My thoughts of the day. If you don't mind."

"I don't mind at all," he promised, beginning to feel a familiar excitement down there.

"Sleeping together, incidentally, was a euphemism, because we'd be fucking not sleeping. We'd be in this hotel on expenses having wine with our dinner, before going up to your room and falling to the bed, tearing off our clothes and five-star fucking. How does that sound?"

"Amazing," he said, "Miraculous, actually."

"I know. Because I know everything about you."

"Everything?"

"The whole story."

"So how does it go? Out of interest."

"In a nutshell: [*In the year of 68 there was a boy born and named Simon, after Simon Templar. His upbringing was happy if unremarkable. He had two brothers, no sisters, which saddened his mother at times because she would've liked a girl to balance things up in the nest. In later life he'd wish the same – if only he'd had a sister, he maintained, he'd be better with women. Because in later life he was a philanderer and serial heart and marriage-breaker. His first marriage to Alison, which yielded all five of his kids, now fledged, ended when she found a note from his lover, whose name was Katie. No mobile phones in those days – incriminating evidence was found in pocketed handwritten receipts and love-letters at the bottom of the drawer containing his work papers, the kind of work papers his wife – in his confident opinion – would never be interested in. His second marriage ended in tragedy when his wife Trudy died in a car-crash, made all the more tragic because she was fleeing the house in rage after discovering another of his long line of infidelities. Simon would of course feel guilty about this, and of course still does. Not least because the post-mortem revealed she was pregnant. His third and current wife, Caroline, whom he married because he needed her more than he loved her and she needed him less than the Church, will inevitably leave him also].* Am I right, Simon?"

Having unravelled his tale and left her remaining morsels of steak and his to go cold, she penetrated him with a look and lipstick smile. Her eyes were blue as jewels, one of which sometimes obscured by the asymmetric fringe she coiled seductively behind her left ear pierced with diamond stud.

"Am I right?" she repeated.

"In a nutshell?"

"Yes."

"Mmm," he admitted, not thinking for one moment that he should ask how she knew all these facts, even with their factual imperfections. He was thinking other matters. "Just one thing. Why will Caroline leave me?"

"You've been up to your old tricks."

"I've been faithful to her," he said, before adding, "Mostly."

"She knows that."

"But how? How would she know anything? I've been very careful."

"Which is interesting. The wife you've least cared about is the one you've most wanted to protect. You know why? A man in his fifties, done well for himself, owes not a penny, not even a mortgage, kids no longer dependent, nice car, a Lexus or something I shouldn't wonder, risen to senior management level, company so fond of him they pay for swanky hotels like this… Looking to retire gracelessly and keep Caroline quiet with a nice church, a nice suburban garden with perennial borders and twice-yearly caravan holiday in Cornwall. All nice and cosy. So why wouldn't he be careful when he does what he's about to do tonight?"

"You're right," he said.

"I'm never wrong."

"Except you are." She cocked her head to one side at this, again wrapping the fallen fringe ear-wards. "My first wife was not, in fact, called Alison, the lover was not, in fact, called Katie. My second wife was not, in fact, called Trudy, who did not die in a car accident and was not pregnant at the time, and Caroline is, in fact, called Carol*ynne*. So a number of shall we say slight inaccuracies?"

"Artistic licence, I should say" she said, and they both laughed, before she went on to qualify, "You said in the conference you'd been married three times *et cetera*. You like to personalise the content where necessary, make the whole thing more human, more engaging because you're one of us. I was just plugging the gaps in your story from the depths of my vivid imagination."

Just then, another voice entered the equation; the waiter asking if they'd finished.

"Yes, thank you," they said, and Simon confirmed that they'd neither of them be requiring pudding and that the tab should be put on Room 968.

When the waiter had taken their plates, she remarked on the room number, saying it was lucky because the digits amounted to twenty-three, the date on which she was born, and that the number twenty-three had many more significances though she wouldn't elaborate. Another time perhaps.

"Another time perhaps," he agreed, enjoying the promised pudding of another time in her company.

"So?" she said.

"So," he said, "I'd very much like it if you'd join me in Room 968."

"OK," she said.

"But first," he said, "Can I ask your name? Only at the conference you didn't wear your lanyard."

"I'm such a maverick," she teased, "hope that doesn't give me a black mark in terms of my joining the company?"

"I like a maverick," he said promptly, "The company needs more mavericks."

"It's Keeley," she said, and without further ado she stood and expected him to do the same…

Room 968 was penthouse, with a private balcony monitoring the starry blackness of London. On it, they sipped the wine he'd carelessly plucked from the daylight robbery minibar. She loved the view, she said, confessing she'd never stayed in such a salubrious place before, and found the room to be sparsely-tasteful in neutral colours. She'd tried all the lights which always baffled Simon with their arbitrariness. She'd explored the bathroom with its bath, shower, bidet and sauna. And finally, she'd sampled the bed for firmness and approved.

"Are you sure about this?" he asked, meeting the London Eye instead of her own blue ones.

"If you are," whispered Keeley, reassuring that if he was nervous then it was fine because she was too, but wouldn't be adding that she doesn't normally do this kind of thing because that would be predictable and as a maverick she was anything but. "But first, take a shower, relax, I'll be waiting."

He would've protested, saying he'd rather just get on with things, but she'd already pecked his lips, a gesture designed to stop them speaking rather than to whet their appetite.

"Don't you think I've got very beautiful lips?" she said.

His answer was to lean in for another kiss, but she held up a hand then pointed to the bathroom.

So Simon, chastened, did as he was asked. The shower was warm, welcome and indeed relaxing. He could hear music through the water and smiled to himself, knowing she'd helped herself to the sound system. She'd be on the bed now, waiting, perhaps in her underwear. He wrapped a towel around him, checking in the mirror his paunch, which wasn't too bad and anyway he could breathe in, hastily combed his thinning hair, kicked on the slippers bearing the hotel logo and padded into the bedroom to join her on the bed.

But she wasn't on the bed, in her underwear, waiting with a smile and soft music. She was gone, along with his wallet. Of course he quickly realised he'd been taken for the fool he was. How could he be so stupid, so naive? What kind of man could be taken in, delude himself that he'd be attractive to a beautiful blonde some twenty years younger? The kind of man he was. After some seconds angrily taking stock of everything lost, and pondering the dangerous folly of drawing attention, he dialled reception to draw attention to the fact that he'd been robbed. But of course it was too late, the girl had gone, and of course the hotel's CCTV had temporarily blipped.

Simon didn't for a moment think he'd sleep that night and didn't for a moment believe the girl would be in attendance at the conference next day – a glance at the list of attendees in his conference notes bore proof – nobody called Keeley. And not for a second could he concentrate on the sessions to follow, which seemed to drag on far longer than the scheduled six hours and seemed to steal his focus entirely, a fact which didn't escape his boss who'd dropped in for the afternoon, in "a purely observational capacity". But that would be another story, the story about his awkward meeting with his boss next day, and his gradual decline in the company pecking-order and eventual redundancy…

Driving home, Simon gripped the steering wheel of his Lexus and worried. What could he tell Carolynne about his wallet? He'd cancelled his cards as a matter of course of course, that was easy, but he knew he'd have to lie to Carolynne that he'd lost his wallet in the hotel bar – a lie not far from the truth, a white lie as he preferred to term it.

As he parked up not entirely square in the drive of his modest rural semi, with Carolynne's immaculate bed of perennials jiving colourfully in the wind, that was what he decided – he'd lost his wallet in the hotel bar while having drinks with his boss, and he didn't want to talk too much about the conference because he was tired and needed an early night because, genuinely, he had a meeting with his boss first thing. And he also vowed that he'd never so much as look at another woman again, young or otherwise. He loved Carolynne and their beautiful house in Surbiton she constantly kept clean and tidy, and her word-search puzzles and Delia cookbooks and her garden and her simple tales of life with the congregation and the fact she rarely bothered him in the sex department...

"Hello, Carolynne," he cheered, as he entered the hall, threw his keys on the console table and shrugged out of his coat, inhaling the smell of a baking pie.

"Hello," returned a voice, which he'd later reflect was a little flatter than usual, just as he'd later reflect that the aroma of cooking was mixed with a faint scent only very vaguely familiar.

Carolynne was in the sitting room, where she'd normally rise to give him a kiss but this time didn't. "How was the conference?" she asked.

"Very good," he said, "I'm worn out though. Afraid I had a bit of a mishap."

"You mean this," she said, holding aloft his wallet. Before he could feign surprise, or ask how on earth that got here, she added, "A young lady called Keeley brought it round. She said she found it in the hotel bar and hoped I didn't mind but she opened it to find an address. I said of course I didn't mind and it was very kind of her to go to the trouble."

"Absolutely!" he managed, suppressing his growing suspicion, "What a kind person and what a relief."

"Dinner's in the oven," she said, rising from the sofa.

"You going out?"

"Church meeting," she said. "It's steak pie – I hope the hotel haven't been feeding you too much steak?"

With creeping unease he watched her head for the door, where she paused, and without turning said, "I know you're lying."

"Pardon?"

"I've seen the letters in your work drawer, the cards, the receipts, and yes I've even seen the distasteful trophies of your deception. I've even seen the texts on your phone. You've been lying to me for a very long time. So we at the church wondered how *you'd* like it."

"I don't follow."

"Very beautiful girl, Keeley, isn't she?" she said, now turning. "Also a very talented member of the Church Players.

Wants to make a career of it, and I think she stands a chance, don't you? Would you say it was a brilliant performance, Simon?"

"Carolynne, please…"

"We laughed so much. About you and your clothes and your farcical attempt at looking young. Breathing in that potbelly of yours. The way you comb what little bit of hair you have left, and yes even take to dyeing it for heaven's sake! You fool!"

"All right we need to sit down and talk."

"You've gone very pale, is everything all right? Perhaps talking's too much, you need a good sleep after your pie."

"Carolynne please…"

"No. I can no longer bear to look at you. I can no longer stand having to pretend I love you, having to pretend I'm happy to go on living with a man as pitiful as you. I can't even bear to watch you eat, the way you suck your teeth, the way you break wind without so much as an excuse me. And as for sleeping beside a pig like you, I shudder to even think of it. I've made up the bed in the spare room. Tomorrow we'll talk about you leaving."

And with those words final and unchallenged by a man on rung one of a horrible downwards spiral, Carolynne calmly closed the door behind her.

*

"I still don't know how I came to be the woman I am," is what is said the night Carolynne meets a young lady for a drink at Bottle Tops, a trendy bar on Chapel Row she never knew existed. The young lady sips her lager, her beautiful eyes glinting effortlessly in a lozenge of light from the ceiling as she coils her lopsided fringe around a studded ear.

"Because you're the woman he turned you into," she suggests with a wan smile. Carolynne has known Keeley for only six months, since the night she first came to Chapel clutching a violin case. Not long graduated she was, back home at her parents' in Surbiton from where she'd be applying for jobs in

London and beyond. A Performing Arts Degree is what she studied and what she passed with distinction and what she hopes will metamorphose into a profession. She'd received good notices in small touring productions as an undergraduate, and heard good noises from theatre practitioners about her chances of success. Most recently she'd played Ange in the Baptist Chapel Players' production of Abigail's Party, to keep her hand in, and brought the house down every night of a four-week run – *"I've got very beautiful lips"* was one line in particular that had them rolling in the aisles. But now, she is having a drink with Carolynne and discussing a role of a different kind that she'd played. At first, Carolynne had grave misgivings about the plot the girl had hatched, but something in the mischievous glint in Keeley's eye had become infectious, persuasive, such was Carolynne's unhappiness at what she found in Simon's work drawer and made her know the marriage was over and she must confront the man who'd made her so unhappy – the man who'd dismissed the notion of children, who'd seen off two previous marriages, one of which ended in tragedy and unanswered questions... Yes if it were to be gauged in financial terms she married well; the man had a good job that paid handsomely, he'd risen through the ranks, afforded them their twice-yearly holiday in Cornwall, their lovely house with its dancing perennials, its modern fitted kitchen and two thousand pound Rangemaster in which she could bake the hundreds of pies and cakes that had without fail, gone down so well at Chapel functions. She'd tried to be the woman he wanted her to be but had failed enough to believe she was at fault. Gradually, however, she'd come to know she didn't love him, could never love him the way he wanted her to and to behave the way he wanted her to...because the week before, she had found the answer to the unanswered questions about the court case and the acquittal and the more besides in the drawer he believed she'd never look in, the drawer in which he'd kept the knickers belonging to one of his tarts.

"How did that make you feel?" Keeley had asked, the night the plan was mooted.

"Honestly?"

"Yes honestly."

"I wanted to swear. I wanted to call him names."

"What names?"

"I wanted to call him a...bastard."

"It's fine to swear. God would've understood."

"Would He have understood what I didn't? The reason I'd become the woman I'd become?"

"He would. Because you do too, in your heart of hearts."

And so it was that Carolynne had found herself in the kitchen with her favourite Delia tome, "How to Cheat at Cooking". As she'd taken her favourite knife, and trimmed the chuck steak into one-inch cubes and the ox kidney even smaller, she'd allowed herself to think about what might be happening at the conference. Had Keeley managed to get through security and infiltrate? Had she made a good impression from the floor? Had she flickered those beautiful eyes at him in the way that would make him think of her in *that* way? Becoming nervous and shaking with unknown excitement, she'd had to be careful not to cut herself. And then to the pastry, she'd sifted the flour with salt, deftly holding the sieve up high to air it, and then added butter and lard and gently rubbed it with her fingertips. She would serve the pie with new potatoes, and broccoli and carrots, and make some extra gravy the way Delia said and the way he liked it.

"In my heart of hearts?" she'd said.

"In your heart of hearts."

While she could not have denied that it felt good, there was still a doubt in the mix as she wondered if God would forgive her. Yet, in her mischievous way, Keeley had given justification, absolution for the crime she believed she was going to commit. And so persuasive was her justification, her absolution, Carolynne had surrendered to the plan.

And now, in Bottle Tops, the trendy bar on Chapel Row she never knew existed, she thinks again of what she found in the drawer, the notes, the knickers, the answers to the unanswered questions asked of the pig she married.

"I simply want to help you," Keeley explains, seeing Carolynne's near to tears and placing her hand on hers, "When I came home and my parents were tearing each other apart, you put me together. You listened when I cried at the Chapel, you paid to have my violin restrung, you put an arm around my shoulder when I felt lonely, you did everything my mother didn't, couldn't. I'm just repaying you for that and hoping you'll get to feel good about it. As for God, frankly who cares? You're a different woman."

"You know I think you're right," says Carolynne, suddenly straightening tall in her chair, "I am a different woman!"

"And does it feel good?" Keeley asks.

"It jolly well does," she says, "I am not the woman he turned me into, I'm the woman who *is*."

"The woman who is?"

"Yes, Keeley, the woman who *is*."

"The woman who is what?"

"The woman who is prepared to bake a pie with additional filling for a start."

"You mean you improvised?" Keeley says, inquisitively coiling her hair behind a studded ear.

"I did. I went off-piste. I added extra ingredients."

"Poison? Four and twenty blackbirds?"

"No," she says with a laugh she can no longer control, "steak, kidney and a pair of knickers that once belonged to a certain tart!"

*

"Last Halloween"

London Road, early hours of the morning, a cold October 2015, not a soul, just a quiet Lucozade-lit road that Keith drove along to where an hour before he'd smashed Ricky Moran's head with a brick. He crossed the railway line and pulled into the disused coal wharf that would in time be sold off to house dozens but was for now a fresh and shallow grave for one.

Keith stopped the car and gathered his thoughts. He knew this place well, he worked here for ten years till he got laid off, the need for solid fuel in people's fireplaces giving way to central heating. He wasn't popular with his workmates but that didn't matter, he didn't remember ever being popular anywhere or any time in his life. But that didn't matter either, he decided, not anymore, because he hadn't long left in this loneliness and anonymity. With that existential thought he turned off the engine and got out to crunch the icy puddles and find what he came back for.

Earlier that night, he'd sat quietly in the corner of the Leopard, sipping a pint, watching and listening to three men at the dartboard. The first, an Englishman called Derek, was regaling a Scotsman called Willy and yes it's true an Irishman called Michael, with stories between throws. The stories were nothing of import or value but rich in fantasy, such as when Derek slept with a prostitute in Amsterdam, the first of hundreds he'd since fucked.

"Does your wife know about all these assignations?" asked Michael, seemingly in awe.

"Of course not!" exclaimed Derek, "And it's going to stay that way or your life's not worth living, mate."

"I'm saying nothing anyway," assured Michael, knowing secretly that if there was a secret to be kept, he was the last person to keep it.

"Me neither," agreed Willy, knowing secretly that if there was a secret to be kept, Michael was the last person to keep it, your man was not to be trusted and then again neither was he, because nobody in the pub world keeps secrets, that's the rule, that's the way it is.

From his quiet corner, Keith took another sip of his pint, knowing secretly that if *anyone* was going to tell Derek's wife he used prostitutes it would be he, Keith. He didn't like Derek Ireson, who once cheated him out of twenty quid in a game of darts, long forgotten by him but not by Keith. Plus he was one of the cruellest bullies at the workplace. Tomorrow perhaps? No, the day after, which happened to be a Sunday when Derek's wife would go to church and pray for those less fortunate. It would have to be Sunday because he was to observe the rule of three victims that with good reason he'd earmarked for this journey of destruction, starting with the next person who darkened the door, and subsequently in order he deemed fitting...

By the time Keith had ordered and half-imbibed his second cider, the three men had been joined by Ricky Moran, a bigshot American who'd come across the pond in the Sixties and made his living breeding racing horses, several of which had been big winners including The Derby and The Grand National. It was no secret in the town that Ricky was rich and the house that stood on the edge of it was as ostentatious as the man who lived in it, who was to be seen flashing his loud suits, shiny jewellery and money around in this pub on a regular basis. It was Ricky to whom Keith had approached about four years ago to ask for a job, having been made redundant when the coal merchants closed, and been turned down, the first in a long line of rejections that kept growing until this day. It was not the rejection itself that got to Keith so much as the manner of it.

"You want me to hire you to muck out stables when you look like *this*?" Ricky had said, "A man looking like he crept out of the garbage can? Who'd scare the horses so much as look 'em in the eye?" And then he'd laughed and told Keith to get out of his face because he had to go eat a burger.

Now, Keith was eking out his pint, watching and listening as Ricky joined Michael, Willy and Derek at the bar, wafting a wad of twenties, and deciding finally that yes, this was the man who was to be first past the finishing post.

Knowing that these nights Ricky always walked from the pub to his home because he lost his licence a while back, and that London Road was the way, Keith silently finished the rest of his pint and slipped out into the frosty night.

Two hours later, Keith was in the living room of 23 Pepper Street, a small terraced house he shared with his mother, making a cup of tea and four slices of toast. Taking these from the cramped dark kitchen into the living room and setting them down on the settee to cool, he then took the bundle of money from his pocket and placed it behind the clock on the mantlepiece, then fished for the bracelet he'd gone back for. Enjoying and smiling to himself at the smoothness of its platinum, he then flicked at a dried map of blood he spotted on his coat, picked up the three darts from the sideboard and threw them hard into the board he'd screwed to the back of the door. Thunk, thunk, thunk. Then he plucked one dart from the cork and with it pinned the bracelet into treble 20.

By now he was tired and hungry and all of a sudden felt the cold. Clicking on the gas fire, he returned to the settee, switched on the TV to catch the Sky Crime docs he'd series-linked, and began to address his meal. Just then, there was the sound from the floor above – thunk, thunk, thunk.

"Coming," he called, but didn't move.

Thunk, thunk, thunk.

"I said I'm coming!"

He knew he'd have to go up, but not yet. First, because for Keith, everything even his mother had to be taken care of in order, he'd finish his supper.

Compared to the large fatted lump of flash American horse-breeder Ricky Moran, Keith's mother was extremely slight and etiolated. Nevertheless, it surprised him how difficult it was to move her. When she was gathered into the sack made from her bedding, she bump, bump, bumped down the stairs like a cumbersome piece of furniture. Luckily, she hadn't made a fuss, just one stifled scream when he crunched her head with the stick she used to beat on the floor to demand attention. After that the only sounds were splashing and Keith's exhalations as he pounded up and down in these hours come day of the dead.

Once downstairs, he put his coat back on and spotted the map of blood from last night, now dry and darkened as innocuous as gravy spilled from a spoon.

The cold air blasted him as he opened the door of the little terraced house he'd shared with her for some twenty years since his father last closed the door behind him. These were the pregnant hours of Saturday morning but they hadn't yet born light, so it was safe to go and open the boot of his car with strategic forward-planning. And then he was back in the house, gathering her up and hauling her over his shoulder like one of the many sacks of coal he once shifted in working days. He let the weight take him down the path and in one skilfully arced movement the bag was in and the boot closed. Surely nobody saw him, though he didn't much care.

He hadn't cared, truth be told, since his father left. Keith senior was a strong, hardworking, gentle and handsome man whose only weakness was the curse of the strong. She never understood him, she never forgave his moods, she hadn't the intelligence to know the man to whom she gave a child she didn't want and a marriage she wanted less. She called him weak, feckless, useless, an excuse of a man. He was none of those things. He worked nights, tough, dirty foundry work, and brought home decent money to buy the things she wanted but were never enough. He'd be home at eight in the morning, face and hands black, have his swill and retire to bed on a belly full of porridge he made himself. While he slept away the hours before his next shift, she'd be plastering her face and out of the house to the Horseshoe, where she was known. Both father and son knew this but never talked about it, not even when Keith junior was arrested for affray after being taunted about it at work – there was just a tacit and embarrassed acknowledgement that he'd had to defend his father's honour. But these things do take their toll and ultimately Keith senior had had enough. After a blazing row and slamming doors, with a nod and a grunt that spoke volumes to his son, he took his cap from its peg in the hall and left the house. Four hours later there was a knock on the door and news that he'd been found in the remote depths of Knutton Wood.

After the funeral, his mother finally broke down and confessed she'd been bad but didn't deserve this. She told Keith she loved him and he said he loved her back and he'd look after her now. But even then he knew that one day he would take her, to stop her from leaving him because everybody left him sometime, that's the way it was. They'd parcelled up his father's clothes and given them to the Heart Foundation shop in town, except for the cap which Keith said he'd like to keep, and hung on the peg where it belonged and still hung there today. The cap and the binoculars were what he kept.

By the time Keith hit London Road, the morning sun had burned off the mist, so as he approached the railway and disused coal wharf he could see the blue flashing lights.

"Morning," said the police officer.

"Morning," said Keith as he wound down the driver-side window, "Wasn't speeding was I?"

"Just routine," said the officer, "not a speed check. Where you heading?"

"Birdwatching."

The police officer nodded, spotting the binoculars Keith always had with him and once belonged to his father on the passenger seat.

"Want to see my licence?" he asked, searching his coat pocket for his wallet and flashing it towards the officer.

"Fine," said the officer, "Bit of a twitcher eh?"

"Not a twitcher," corrected Keith, "Twitchers go out on a tip-off. Birders like me just do it random like."

"Thanks for putting me straight," said the officer, perfunctorily.

"I go up there most weekends," added Keith, "Knutton Wood."

"Rather you than me on a cold day like this."

"Has there been an accident?" Keith nodded towards the open-doored ambulance.

"Early days."

"So am I good to go?"

"Yea, you're good. Have a nice time 'birding' or whatever you call it."

An hour later, having done what he'd come to do, Keith was on the edge of Knutton Wood, looking through the 8x30 bins that used to belong to his father, down on the town beyond Moran's suburban acres to where the railway line sliced the countryside in two. He could just about pick out the flashing lights in the distance and wondered if by now the body had been found and the family informed they'd be spending Christmas minus a husband and father. As a precaution he pondered returning home by the other route, where he could call at the supermarket for the provisions he needed for tomorrow's roast dinner. After one final look back towards the spot he'd meticulously chosen to lay his mother to rest with the ghost of the man she in his eyes killed, he returned to his car.

As he pulled in to Pepper Street where at No. 23 he knew he'd have to vigorously clean, he could see Mrs Hales, the widow in 25, knocking at the door. Seeing him pull up, she came down the path to greet him.

"Been out?" she said.

"No shit," Keith said to himself, lugging his shopping bags from the back seat. "Birdwatching. Called at the supermarket on the way back."

"Yes, I saw you leave early. Only I've been knocking for your mother," she said.

"Probably asleep," he said.

"She's all right I take it?"

"Doctor said she's doing well."

"Well, if she needs anything…" said Mrs Hales.

"Thanks," he said, in conclusion.

Inside, he back-heeled the door closed behind him and headed down the gloomy hall where his father's cap still hung and into the kitchen to dump the shopping. Then he moved to the living room, where he thunked another dart into the board, pinning his mother's bracelet along with the other in treble 20. Mrs Hales would be a problem and it irked him to know that, it upset the balance, his rule of three. But first things first, everything in its order, everything right, everything in its place. Tomorrow, while the beef was in the oven, he'd go to the church where Philipa Ireson liked to go and pray for those less fortunate, and give her the devastating news that her husband Derek has been using prostitutes.

No. 23 stank of bleach and Keith hated it more than mess itself, but in these circumstances, he was forced to deem it a necessary evil. Cleaning up the house was a huge undertaking and his hands were red raw and freezing cold – the four-bar gas fire in the living room barely able to take away the breath he saw wisping in front of him. If his belly had anything inside he would chuck up, sickened as he was at the cold comeuppance he'd served before the painstakingly disinfected dessert. But he'd been running on empty since the four slices of toast that had passed through him in the early hours of Saturday morning. It was now Sunday and the thought of the rich smell then taste of succulent meat excited him, taking the edge off his nausea. A Sunday treat to follow the next trick in his weekend of destructive vengeance.

Rising still clothed from the settee he'd made his bed, he entered the kitchen and took the joint from the fridge. Carefully so as not to spill, he freed it from its wrapper, swilled it with warm water, placed it in the tray and slotted it in the oven, turning the gas to 4 for it to slowly cook. By the time he'd done his work, he considered, it would be time to peel the vegetables and get them on the boil. Packaging had always irked him, so the bloody mess on the side had to go straight out to the wheelie bin in the yard. As he ventured out to do the deed, he checked the feeder for sunflower hearts and saw it had barely been touched. He'd for ever yearned a garden with trees and shrubs, a slice of the countryside for the birds he loved, and this pitiful concrete postage stamp that would bring in only the odd house sparrow *Passer domesticus* or occasional blue tit *Cyanistes caeruleus* got him down, and Mrs Hales' irritating opinion that feeding the birds encourages vermin never did much to help.

"How is she this morning?" she asked, intercepting him at the garden gate.

"She's fine," said Keith.

"Am I to fetch her some dinner later?"

"That won't be necessary thanks."

"Are you sure?"

"I bought a bit of topside yesterday," he said.

"Terrible business up at the Wharf," she said, "They're saying it's murder."

Keith had no idea whatsoever of religion, he just didn't get it. One day when they were out birding in the woods his father had asked if he wanted to attend Sunday School like the other kids, but he'd shaken his head – five days a week at normal school was enough for him to be convinced by teachers and pupils alike that he was a bastard and a misfit who'd never amount to much and never be much use to anyone – and his father had only nodded and let the matter rest as he spotted a jay *Garrulus glandarius* in his 8x30 bins. So as he entered St Mary's he wasn't sure what to do, but took with muted thanks as a matter of course the pamphlet he was offered and found his pew. The service had already started, the vicar telling his flock something or other about the clocks going back and trying to make out it gave all those present one more hour to thank God for. Or at least that's how it sounded to Keith, who was only half-listening if listening at all. He was there for other matters than an extra hour with God. Scanning the room and its forty or so throng, he eventually picked out Philipa Ireson, sitting three rows in front of him then rising as bade for the first hymn, *He Who Would Valiant Be.*

Rising himself for no other reason than to remain inconspicuous, Keith looked at the pamphlet and followed the words. It seemed to him that most of the noise was coming from the piped choir against the paucity of the warblers among the pews. Nevertheless he searched the words for meaning

Who so beset him round
with dismal stories
do but themselves confound
his strength the more is.
No foes shall stay his might;
though he with giants fight,
he will make good his right
to be a pilgrim

but by the time he'd fathomed anything it was time to sit down again.

He'd intended to remain for the entire service and speak to Philipa outside, but after stretching his legs for the hymn he realised it was beginning to drag, the murmuring voices at the front punctuated by several rounds of coughing, and Keith was wondering if he'd just give up the ghost on this one and make a quiet and dignified exit. But suddenly there was a moment he saw his chance, when the forty of them were invited to something called *Greeting*, and given the dearth of their numbers they were asked to *greet* as many of their kindred spirits as possible. Though never a tactile person – that wasn't the language of his upbringing – he found himself hugging those around him and beyond, and whispering words in the ear of the person he came to see: "At school you called me Gypsy," he said unto her, "Ask Derek if he's "travelled"."

Two hours later, Keith was parked in Oak Bank Close with his binoculars, viewing Derek's neatly topiarised house a hundred yards away, and watching the man leave the premises and slam into his car, looking grim and no doubt fresh from an interrogation and row with his wife and hopefully the first of many leading to a painful and costly divorce. Keith replayed the potential narrative in his head; she asking what that gypo meant when he said what he said in the greeting, he saying he didn't know what she was on about, she pressing him and, amid the ensuing row, he letting something incriminating slip, before slamming out and driving off no doubt towards the Leopard to find out which of his bastard friends spilt the beans, the Irishman or the Scotsman?

Arriving back at No. 23, where he knew the beef was ready to baste, Keith was once again door stepped by Mrs Hales.

"I'm very worried about her now," she said, and he knew this wasn't going away. "I've knocked on three times."

And it was in this moment that Keith, with some irritation, had confirmation that there'd have to be a fourth dart.

"I told you, she's fine. Come in and see for yourself."

Afterwards, Keith peeled the veg as planned, put them to boil, then took the dart and pinned a third piece of jewellery into treble 20 before sitting in his bloody cold living room to reconcile.

All his life he'd been told he was useless, he'd never prosper, he'd never be anyone. They said he smelled, that he was disruptive, destructive even, cruel because he stole birds' eggs, blew them and stored them labelled in a box along with butterflies pinned. But for Keith, as he gazed icily at the blood-splattered room and the sleeping woman who lived alone and wouldn't be missed, this was not destruction, this was not cruel at all. His work had been painstakingly and impeccably methodical, *con*structed and executed. And now it was finished, or nearly, he'd be someone. He'd be talked about, written about and read about, celebrated and reviled, he'd be named, and shamed no doubt, but named, in files and possibly scrap books of those who followed. He'd forever be linked to a place on the map where people would say these things simply didn't happen in a sleepy town like this. Thinking back to the church service and the hymn he hadn't sung, he tried once again to relate to the words therein, and supposed it was true – all his life he'd fought with giants and perhaps now his fight was over he'd be making good his right and heading to a special place. Because after the roast dinner, and after he'd viewed all the programmes nature and crime that he'd series-linked, he had one last trick to perform. No need for cleansing the house this time, no requirement of bleach. He would thunk a final dart, don his father's cap, check the mirror in the hall and tell himself he was someone, then go to Knutton Wood, take his binoculars deep into its dark canopy where his father hung and fashion a noose with the strap.

*

"Embers"

David watched as news spread like televisual wildfire from the corner of his living room; flashing images of people fleeing for their lives, charred remains of homes, burnt-out cars and some of those bereaved interviewed at the scene unfolding, he thought insensitively and certainly sensationally. At that time, the official death toll was seventy-four. It filled him with horror and sadness but at the same time made him think.

In nineteen-seventy-four, David was at Manchester Grammar, a bright fifth-year student with his sights on a career in law. A place at Oxbridge was accurately predicted by staff and pupils alike. One of those, a sixteen-year-old Diantha, equally clever and stunningly beautiful, was David's girl. They were never apart, kissing often like first-time lovers do, hand in hand around the grounds, laughing together, playing together and studying together. Peers would say they were joined at the hip, they'd never be apart, they'd end up at the same university, walk the same career path and one day down the aisle. Cynics would say she would get pregnant too soon. Neither were correct. David did indeed read at Cambridge while Diantha went to Edinburgh, where her Greek father lived. At first the two of them would speak to each other every day, write long letters saying how much they pined for that 'first time' back again, and sometimes spend weekends together when he or she had enough spare time or money. And then, one day, David met Kay…

While many, not least her father, predicted Diantha would see out her three years at Edinburgh, pass with honours and go on to Masters and even beyond, it didn't work out like that. Because when David met Kay, Diantha changed. She began to find more interest in music, especially rock, and the once beautiful dark young girl gradually metamorphosed into a

Goth, no less beautiful but well and truly Goth, so by year three of her degree she'd pretty much dropped out. Much of the time she spent listening to her Walkman, hanging out with friends, smoking pot, travelling occasionally down to Whitby to find peace at the Abbey or going to gigs in Leeds, Liverpool and Manchester. Killing Joke, The Cure, Siouxsie, Sex Gang Children... Her father wasn't happy, he strongly felt she was being led astray and said so, and they'd fight. He sometimes phoned his ex-wife in London to remonstrate about their daughter but she said she's a grown woman, she can do her own thing...like *he* did before they got divorced. Defeated and chastened, and anyway off his feet with the successful restaurant he owned, Diantha's father left Diantha to it, though secretly prayed that in time she'd grow up, grow out of it and return to university.

When she was twenty-one and barely on speaking-terms, Diantha moved out of her father's house and in with some friends, drifting from part-time dead-end jobs to nothing at all to eat. But her father was right...in time, like many things and many people, Diantha changed again, to someone wanting more from life than that, in other words a husband and a child. She realised that though in the company of many friends almost all the time, she felt deep down a loneliness almost all the time. And so came the hour when she decided to settle down, and the time when she metamorphosed back to the beautiful, slim and neatly-dressed woman that was always the real her. She didn't want to go back to university, that ship had left the dock, an ordinary life became more attractive, an ordinary life and an ordinary job that might not pay too well but it was money earned along with pride, respectability and simplicity. Which is how we would then find her in a flower shop, where she'd remain for more than thirty years, starting part-time, going full-time, working up to manageress and finally, having saved and saved, buying the business outright as a going concern and winning back the respect and love of her father. And which is where, in 2018, David would find her too...

"But how?" she exclaimed, hands covering her face in shock.

"I knew you'd gone to Edinburgh of course," David said, "so as good a place to start as any. I saw your father through the window in his restaurant, he still looks well, so I hoped you were there too. But you weren't, so I was heading back to the station and saw your name above the shop."

It was true, when she'd bought the previous owner out, she'd re-branded the florists' and called it by her name. "Eponymous Diantha," he said.

"Sounds Greek," she said with a laugh.

"Sounds like a flower," he said, earnestly.

By now they were in a sleek bar, lunching, catching up, laughing, joking, reminiscing, clasping hands in disbelief at all those years that passed between them and made him grey but not aged her hair or indeed skin in the slightest, and he marvelling that her face now was the same face that smiled over at him in the classroom in nineteen-seventy-one. English, he believed it was.

"I saw the news and thought of you," he said, "I had this horrible notion you were there, caught up in it all."

"I've only been back to Athens twice in all this time," she said ruefully, "Daddy goes sometimes to see his brothers, my uncles. It's so sad what's happening."

"They're all OK I hope?" he said, remembering them all because he and Diantha once went on holiday there when they were students.

"Daddy heard from them. He was very worried. I told him not to, they'd be fine. He gave me a hug, for the first time in years. We haven't always got on that well."

"Is that down to your rebellious nature?"

"Me? Rebellious?" she said, smiling widely with those teeth a beacon against the olive skin.

"You were so intelligent," he said.

"Are you saying I am not now? That I could've done so much more with my life than sell flowers?"

"I'm not saying that at all," he said, "the shop is beautiful, successful it would appear?"

"I don't do too bad," she said, "the weather is so hot, some people are afraid of buying flowers because they die too soon."

"Like those people I saw on the news," he said, "Dying too soon."

There was a sombre pause at that, the first in their conversation since they sat down to lunch, and in which they ate a few more bites. And then he looked at her and took a sip of wine and said, "I didn't think of you just because of the news. I've thought about you a lot."

"Me too," she said, and then described how she'd dropped out of university since they lost touch and, sensing this was a pointed remark, he said he was sorry how things turned out.

"Sorry?" she said, "You're not sorry you met Kay."

"No," he said, "sorry about what I did to you."

"Did you marry her?" she asked.

"I never married," he said, "No kids either. She and I fizzled out if I can put it like that. Last I heard she'd moved to America. Boston I think."

"And you lost touch?"

"Yes."

"Just like you lost touch with me. A theme in your life."

"Which is true," he said, "I can't deny there have been others. And I can't deny they were never more than ephemeral relationships."

"Have you never lived together with a woman?"

"Oh yes. One or two, but things never worked out for one reason or another."

"One reason or another being David Millington," she said, smiling into her wine glass and peering over it with those beautiful brown eyes.

"What about you? Ever married? Kids?"

"Me?" she said, "I also had many boyfriends, mostly when we lived in communes, great fun at the time but awfully fucking sad when I look back."

"And recently?" he said.

"Recently…" she said and tailed off. He saw a moistness in her eyes now, and while part of him wanted to push for

102

more, part of him didn't for fear of stoking something un-pleasant which would sadden him as much as her, and he was somehow relieved when the waiter appeared to take their plates.

"Thanks," she said.

"Would you like the dessert menu?" the waiter asked.

"Love to," she said, "but I need to get back"

"So soon?" said David.

"Sophie's young. She's very good with customers but sometimes not so great with the till, if you know what I mean."

"I do," he said. Then, as the waiter returned with the bill, she noticed David's wallet—a black leather Pierre Cardin that she'd bought him as a gift when he got the grades to get into Cambridge.

"You still have it? All this time," she remarked.

"I do," he said, "Bit dog-eared now, but yes. Sometimes I find myself trying to add up all the amounts that have come and gone in all this time. If I still had it I'd be a millionaire I suppose."

"I always thought you would be anyway," she said, "A millionaire I mean."

As they blinked their way out of the bar into the bright afternoon sun, he looked at the woman Diantha had become. Tall, slim, immaculately-dressed, long dark hair tied with a fiery yellow bow to match the flowers on her maxi-dress and the ones in her window. She was as beautiful today as she always was. And he loved her like he always did, the kind of love that got there first but which got to the ticker tape before they were old enough to understand what love is.

"David," she said, turning to him on the pavement, "Why did you come?"

He paused for a while. He'd thought about the 'why' many times over the past two days since watching that news bulletin, and while there were many reasons, curiosity, nos-talgia, impulse, it always came back to that one word, love. But it wasn't the word he could say right now, because the years somehow erased it, she needed to get back to work and somehow and heart-breakingly it didn't seem appropriate. So instead he simply said, "Because I wanted to see if you were still as beautiful as you were in the past."

"And am I?" she asked.

"You are," he said, "In fact I'd say more so."

"Thank you. And now I must go."

"But will we see each other again?"

And she closed her wonderful eyes, shook her head and said, "David you're as beautiful today as you were in the past also. Perhaps it's best if we left it all there. Memories."

"Sure," he said, softly, "But please, at least take my card."

As he fingered again into that wallet, she hesitated for a few agonising seconds, before taking the card he proffered, then kissing him on both cheeks and turning her back to head down Princes Street.

On the train back to London David switched his mobile on and filed through the many missed calls and messages. Some of them were nuisance, others were important work things, including one or two relating to the Athens fire. Not that he would ever need it, the fire too would always be a reminder. There was nothing yet from Diantha. And as the train hummed smoothly through Berwick and the stunning Northumberland coast lit and shadowed by glorious sun, the brilliant heatwave that had caused people here to head for the sea and taken others elsewhere to their death, and wilted many a bunch of flowers, he thought about her all the time and the face that was almost the same as the one that smiled back at him in the classroom in nineteen-seventy-one. He wanted to know why she'd cried when he asked what had happened recently and wanted to reach out and hold her. He wanted to know so many things that filled the years they shouldn't have lost and for which he'd regret. But he may never know. No, there was nothing from Diantha.

*

Next morning, David was about to leave his Clapham home for work when there was a knock on the door, which he opened to find a man holding a bunch of lilies. "David Millington?" the man said. Surprised, he thanked the man, took them inside and put them in a vase, the only vase he owned which in truth was a pint glass stolen from some bar on the high street when out on a colleague's stag do he'd really wanted to avoid and couldn't. In separating the stems from the wrapping he discovered an envelope, which contained a handwritten note. He knew the writing instantly. It was Diantha's. And it read:

Oh David why did you come back into my life at this time? It was so lovely seeing you again and I meant it when I said that you are still a beautiful man. You said it was not just because of what you saw on the news about the wildfires in my homeland, that you thought about me a lot. But if it <u>was</u> the fires that made you actually come and find me then it's one good thing of the many good things that will come of tragedy. You're one phoenix from the flames. I have also thought about you a lot through these years. You know I loved you once with all of my heart and I sensed you wanted me to be that woman again, but sadly I can't, I cannot love you in that way now. You see it would not be fair to fall in love again, on myself or on you. We talked about so many things in the short time we had, almost like the years never happened, but I didn't talk about one thing. I am selling my business and going back to Athens with Daddy, where I will stay until I die. The Doctors said it won't be long, months or even weeks. So that is the choice I have made. If I can also help in some way the people I know who have suffered during the fires, people I know who have lost someone close, that will be another good thing to come from this. I will say goodbye to you now, and ask forgiveness for not being able to see you again. I send these lilies with my fondest wishes and hope you like them and they don't die too soon! David there will always be a place in my heart for you and I truly wish you continued success and future happiness.
   'agapó gia pánta'
   Diantha x

David put the note down on his desk and sank to the chair in front of it. He was shaking. It was early yet he needed a drink. It was a lot to take in and he knew he'd have to read the note again and again. He was due in court at ten, a murder case, but how could he focus today of all days? How could he stand for the defence of someone he knew was guilty of evil, when someone so good was being prematurely taken? Why do bad things happen to innocent and beautiful people undeserving of such pain? Like the people in Athens, twenty-six of them huddled together to die, showing love and support for each other while at the mercy of the flames. Why these things could happen he had no idea, like he had no idea what to do about the letter. She'd written so much but said so little, so many questions needing to be asked – what was her illness? How long had she *actually* got? Was she in pain? Was there really nothing anyone could do? And finally, most heartbreaking of all, how could he ever accept there was really nothing *he* could do?

*

"I Am the Egg Man"

Walter was putting out plates while two eggs boiled, one for himself and one for his brother Andrew, not too soft not too hard. The kitchen of their farmhouse was cold and damp and the boiling of the eggs made it impossible to see outside. In the steamed-up window he made a porthole then peered out on the misty morning, and could just about make out the grounds of the smallholding where the chickens were already milling, clock-working their way around and scratching the earth for grubs. Their ramshackle of sheds looked gloomy in the distance, which made Walter feel sad. He looked back at Andrew who was sitting at the table ready, and served him his egg with the soldiers he'd neatly cut. This was the morning routine, observed as strictly and predictably as any new day itself would follow night.

They ate in silence and this was the norm too, because Andrew had given up talking, in fact he hadn't spoken in almost a year. Not that Walter bothered, in truth the prolonged manly silences suited him, it was the words of a woman he craved. Andrew was dressed as usual in his overalls, not because he was regimental about being dressed early but because he never took them off, even for his bed. If Andrew could talk they'd discuss the fact that the diggers would be coming today, but he couldn't, so they didn't, so Walter was alone with his thoughts.

He'd booked in the diggers the week before and they'd said yes they'd start today, a Monday, and it would take them two days, then they'd be ready for the concrete mix. This would form the footings of the new shed they'd been arguing about for years, when Andrew would talk and was able to apply for planning, and that being granted, in order to expand their egg business, which Walter now ran single-handed because Andrew was no longer fit and able. No longer talking.

It all started four years ago when he began to forget things or become confused about detail, and when their conversation ceased to contain foundation. First sign was when he was driving out to Rigg on the Thursday round, and came back saying it was done, but Walter discovered the van was still full of eggs.

"I thought you said it was done," he said.

"It is," said Andrew.

"Then how is it the eggs are still in the van?"

They'd fought about it, Walter calling him a fucking idiot, and come to blows, as was their way of dealing with matters. Walter prided himself on the eggs being fresh so in his view this load was not; by the time Andrew returned to Rigg they'd be off, so they'd have to let the market down that day and cut their losses. They were saving up to build his precious new sheds and this wouldn't help, he'd said.

And things got gradually worse, so much so that it was up to Walter alone to make deliveries, making trips of up to one hundred miles round, every day come hail or shine while Andrew sat in his room. Then one day when Walter returned, his brother wasn't there, found later roaming the town. One day soon after that he roamed over fourteen miles and had to be returned by the police. Once he was missing for three days and searches went out, even a helicopter costing the tax-payer fortunes was mooted, before he suddenly reappeared having slept three nights with the birds. "He's eighty-six," the doctor had said, "He's bound to be forgetful." And that was taken as read.

The business belonged to their father Herbert and before that his father also Herbert and so on. It was a family concern going back generations, the house and its fifteen acres worth millions in the current climate and Walter knew it. He dreamed of selling up and buying a modest house with garden and retiring peacefully like that. He dreamed of it every night, of resting, spending his days in the garden, just sitting, reading, even writing, indulging his love of poetry and perhaps his love of women. But none of this had been possible because Andrew maintained they should honour the family tradition and keep the business going. Walter had argued there was nobody after them to leave it to, so they could sell up now, its value augmented by the new sheds, and reap the rewards, allow some other family to take over; the legacy after all was theirs, the new family might even keep the brand that was known and trusted. Retire and rest, both of them, in peace after a lifetime of toil. But no, Andrew had dug his heels in – it was in both their names when their father signed it over and without two signatures to the contrary, things would remain as they were. The new construction would go ahead and its added value enjoyed; Walter would have to lump it, and lump it he did.

When they'd finished their eggs and drunk their tea, Walter collected the plates and put them in the sink, where the debris of the day before and the day before that were piled unwashed. He'd get round to doing them, but only when he'd time, because he knew Andrew wouldn't do them, he'd simply go back up to his room and sit, thinking God knew what. The condensation had cleared from the windows and Walter looked out, the mist now burned off by the morning sun, the chickens doing what they did, oblivious, happy, hungrily scratching. He would go out soon, shoo them to the next paddock and feed them there before the diggers came, but first he needed to move his bowels. He turned from the window and saw that Andrew was picking his nose which made him feel sick, and eating it which made him feel sicker.

After feeding the chickens and loading the unliveried Transit they'd driven for years, Walter drove down the long lanes into town and rested on the only free car park there was. The day was still cold but his hands were warm, throbbing like his heart. He was thinking of the will. Since Andrew got sick, Walter had invested in a computer, teaching himself how to use it, how to get broadband, how to research, and as far as he understood it he'd have to wait seven years… Looking at himself in the rear-view mirror, he saw he was still young enough, fit, strong, handsome enough were it not for the blepharitis and a cowlick that depressed him, much younger than his brother, some twenty years in fact, and still able to work, make money. Still able to get a woman, make a life with her, if he were given half a chance. With that in his mind he got out of the van and crossed the road into the police station and told them it had happened again.

After the long drive and deliveries to markets, Walter then returned down the quiet lanes to the smallholding, where two men, one fat one thin, were standing smoking by a Bobcat trencher and admiring their work thus far.

"All right?" said the fat one.

"Hello," said Walter.

"We made a start," said the thin one, "Your brother said it was OK."

"My brother?" said Walter.

"The bloke in overalls," said the fat man.

As the trencher got kicked up again, Walter went inside and found Andrew sitting at the table, and asked if he'd spoken to the builders. But Andrew didn't answer, he just stared vacantly and nodded, then shuffled back to the stairs.

"It wasn't my brother," said Walter to the men outside, "It was someone else I know. I don't know where my brother is at this moment in time. I've had to report him missing."

"Right," they said indifferently.

While the men resumed their work, Walter made sure the birds were still happy in the next yard where the older sheds stood, then headed back to the house. He needed to dig out some paperwork.

By the end of the next day, the footings had been dug. It was a cold and wintry evening and the ground was hard beneath his boots when he took the shovel from the barn. But just as he was about to dig a couple of feet deeper than the Bobcat did, he saw a beam of light and heard the crunching of wheels on the drive around the front. Returning to the house, he saw two frosted figures through the window of the door.

"Police," they said, and Walter opened to admit two men, tunics glowing bright in the dim light from the hall. In the kitchen, Walter reluctantly but diligently made cups of tea, apologising for the pile of pots in the sink, as they sat at the table, asking questions about his brother and scribbling in their pads. How long did he say he was missing this time? How many times had this now happened? Had he searched the grounds because last time he was found with the chickens was he not? Did he have a recent photograph? Had he considered a home? It was cold in the kitchen and Walter could see their breath, but he was sweating, from the dig, from his fear of what they'd find upstairs, and from the sound of a barking dog outside. "Fox," he said, "Fucking thing's been bothering the birds. I was out there trying to scare it away as you arrived."

"I'm a townie myself," said one of the officers, as if to explain he couldn't envisage such problems.

"Me too," said the other, "I wouldn't know a fox if I fell over one." At last, the police had all their answers and reassured him they'd do everything they could and not to worry, people like Andrew often turn up eventually. They'd even contact all the hospitals and get a helicopter—if and only if it became absolutely necessary. Thanking them profusely and saying he was very worried this time, Walter let them out, before resuming his moonlit work.

Next morning was greeted by a milky sun with promise of the arrival of spring, as Walter cleared the sink of dishes, boiled an egg, not too hard not too soft, and waited for the concrete.

A week later, the foundations had now gone off and the contractors were due, to start building the first new chicken shed, the one which he and Andrew had come to blows over many times when he had his faculties, which in his opinion was worth building because of the value it would add if and only if they ever came to sell up.

Walter had always been the more sensitive of the two brothers, the one prone to nostalgia and depression, the one who always missed his father Herbert, who'd built this family empire bigger than his ancestors. A fine, strong man with principles even in business. His funeral, many years ago, was a huge affair, it felt like the whole town had come out to pay its respects to the man, and at the wake there was talk of a statue erected in the square, which never happened but to Walter even the talk of it meant that it was there. Herbert was deeply proud of both his sons and, Walter reckoned over his egg, he'd still be proud today, proud of how he and Andrew had taken the business forward, proud of the new shed when erected, proud that he, Walter, had now spared Andrew any more pain. This was how he decided to reconcile what he'd done. The brother he once had, had become nobody, something sitting in the kitchen for his meals then shuffling to the stairs to spend his days in his room thinking God knew what, if thinking at all. The brother who was once handsome, fit and strong just like their father, the brother who was hardworking and passionate, but now no more. The sensitive side of Walter somehow missed him. Once across the table was this other man, eating, talking, making plans, arguing, sometimes vying to bare knuckle fight Walter or the world. Even recently, when the man was essentially gone, he was still there, eating meals, picking his nose and eating that too, and though it made Walter feel sick, at least he was there. And now there was an empty space, just one plate put out, just one egg to boil. But the sensitive side of Walter also reconciled that the man who was once so strong then wasn't, was lost, anguished, bewildered, in pain, suffering. He'd been doing so for years, since that first day when he said he'd made the deliveries but came back with the Transit they'd driven for years still full. For years he'd been on a downwards trajectory, yes for years he'd been suffering. And the thought of that answered Walter's question, that one day he would kill for the company he once had. And then, once he was free, he would with a heavy heart sell the business that Herbert built, get himself a house and a woman to put in it. And he reconciled that even that would make his father proud.

After rinsing the pots, Walter went round with the chicken feed then to load the van before driving into town.

"Any sign?" asked the old woman in the market.

"Nothing," said Walter.

"I'm sure Andrew will be fine," she said, sighing and stroking his hand, "He'll show up again like nothing happened. Just like he always does. I'll take half a dozen."

"Yes, I'm sure."

But in the police station Walter was less sure, and the officers who came to the house last week were talking respectfully about this now causing grave concern. A helicopter was mooted again, as it was becoming more apparent that this would be absolutely necessary.

It was a nice afternoon in town after that; Walter shopped at Tesco for the food he liked and a microwave that would save him time, he walked down the high street to the square where the statue to his father would've been and in fact in his imagination *was*, he looked in estate agents' windows at the kind of house he dreamed of retiring to, he even thought about buying a television but resisted for now. He had his computer for entertainment, and his poetry books.

When the work was done, Walter returned to the smallholding, where a large truck was in the back yard and girders were being craned into place. There was drilling into the concrete, steel framing erected. Walter watched for a while, spoke to some of the men, who said they'd have this finished within the allotted time. Everything was grand, tickety-boo he thought was the phrase one of them used.

In the house he ventured into his brother's room, only the second time he'd done so in probably twenty years or more. He left the bed unmade as Andrew had abandoned it, the mattress cambered where the man had slept, but righted the chair that evidenced his struggle. After washing and shaving, he looked at himself in the mirror – still young enough, fit, strong, handsome, the blepharitis and the cowlick that depressed him having a rare day off. Craving a woman.

By the time the men had called it a day, the steel framing of the first new shed was already huge, magnificent, a statue and monument to those who'd worked so hard down the years. But Walter wouldn't dwell for long, he was the man dressed in his suit, the only one he owned, like a new man, having a walk to the village pub a mile away, one that would be busy, where people knew the gypsy egg man and he knew them, and could ask if anybody had seen his brother, and could have a few pints, perhaps a Jamesons, definitely a conversation. Where possibly he could one day find his bride. As he headed for the yard gate, he saw it was a nice evening, warmer now, the trees in bud, the birds coupling therein and singing – all the sights and sounds of spring interrupted only by the sound of a helicopter in the distance and heart-beating its way through the sky.

*

"It's That Old Evil Called
Love Again"

Two people, one a man the other a woman, were having a drink in a hotel in the South of England surrounded by vineyards. He'd seen her drinking alone and looking nice, tall, slim, brunette, attractive, so he'd positioned himself at the bar where she could see him and ordered a chardonnay. As he'd sipped it, enjoying its cool tang and complimenting its legs and citrusness to the barman almost as if he were a connoisseur, they'd exchanged looks, he and the woman, and smiled. Now, one hour later, here they were, talking, getting to know each other over a second bottle. She was saying she was here on business, been in a conference all day but none of her colleagues wanted to drink that evening hence she was alone, and worked in sales for the company who'd hosted the conference, and lived in Manchester so was staying till tomorrow when she'd do the four-hour drive back. And he was saying what a coincidence because he was also here on business and was also in sales and was also staying till tomorrow when he too would make the four-hour trip back to Manchester. In other words, he was saying, they had so much in common, and she was agreeing in so far as it was indeed a funny thing. And so, the two were getting along fine, and as time and the bottle wore on, the sexual chemistry was more evident and this conversation too had legs. There is absolutely nothing unusual about this story at all, except for the fact that the two people were, in fact, married, and to each other.

Coming to the vineyard was his suggestion during one of their counselling sessions designed to explore the idea of putting back some sparkle into their sex life therefore marriage –

he'd even joked that they could bring back the spark with some sparkling wine, and she'd laughed out of duty, as had the counsellor but out of professional politeness. The counselling had been *her* suggestion, because they'd been married twenty years and the union had gone from youthful excitement and naive exuberance to childlessness and inevitable aridity. In previous sessions they'd decided they were both culpable in different ways for growing apart, and growing apart was something they'd been doing for many years; the night they'd first slept in separate rooms for example was an idea so far back that neither could remember who first pitched it. But in that session, when he'd made his joke about sparkle and the counsellor had laughed out of professional politeness, she'd laughed out of duty and consented to the idea. So here they were, and to the observer it would seem, getting along fine. Internally, however, he was thinking he really did love her, with her love of the soaps and her cushions and scented candles and Maeve Binchy and the looks she'd managed to hold on to, and she was thinking the man wasn't all that to look at and though he was prone to moodiness and internet gratification and essentially selfish, he had some kindness in his heart, along with an admission that he'd been at times difficult to live with. This idea of a 'quasi first date' was a good one, with its added ingredient of wine-tasting, which was addressing the charge she'd made that he'd grown predictable, non-experimental, which was surprising given his propensity to visit certain sites on the internet. So when she excused herself to visit the ladies' and gave him the smile he just about remembered, he grew in confidence that this *was* worth trying and one of the two rooms he'd booked to give authenticity to the fantasy, would be unslept-in that night.

With a degree of excitement, the woman entered the bathroom and checked herself in the mirror, before slipping into a cubicle and clanging the door behind her, then weeing with the thickness she used to in days gone by and was pleased at this sign. When wiped, she sorted the underwear chosen and purchased for the occasion, then left the cubicle and checked for a second time the woman in the mirror – the red and bloated lips and the apple hue of youth to a face she'd worried was fading – before heading back to the bar.

But then, she saw another person outside a room about to go in, smiling at her. It was the smile she saw on the person to whom she'd been talking in the bar some moments before the man had come in. The smile of a woman telling her she was here alone, just giving herself a well-earned weekend break and going with the flow, see what happens type-thing.

Back in the bar, the man was thinking his wife was a long time, but mused she'd be touching up her make-up, making herself beautiful for him, perhaps changing into sexy underwear she'd purchased for the occasion. He'd finish his wine then retire to 'his' room and wait, or she might indeed have beaten him to it and would therefore be waiting outside the door.

But, in another room on another wing of the hotel, the woman was tasting something she'd never known before, with the person to whom she'd been talking in the bar before her husband came in. The person who was giving herself a well-earned weekend break to go with the flow and see what happens type-thing. The taste she was having, she'd often thought and read about in books her husband called Chick-Lit but she preferred Up-Lit, the kind of taste that was right now giving her much more than she'd ever known, the kind of taste that had made her feel the way she felt in the bathroom. Tender, soft and not over in a flash, and not fuelled by sleazy internet gratification.

Back in 'his' room, the man, who'd realised his wife wasn't in fact waiting outside the door, was becoming impatient and frustrated and visiting the site on his tablet that he'd vowed never to visit again on account of coming here with his wife to try and restore some real and not virtual love and excitement.

By now, in the other room on the other wing, the woman was lying with the other person tasting a cocktail of pleasure and guilt, whispering that this had been unexpected, tentatively treading fruit both strange and nice, yet vowing never to do this kind of thing again as she'd agreed to come here with her husband to try and restore some in his words sparkle but in her eyes love. But had they tried? Did she even *want* to try? Had she any love to restore?

"You've been a long time," said her husband when she found him.

"Sorry," she said, and added as per the rehearsed excuse, "I went for some air, I didn't feel well."

"You do look a bit red," he said, "Having one of your hot flushes?"

She left that unanswered.

"Come to bed," he said.

"I don't want to. I think I need more air."

"You need a lie down."

"Please don't tell me what to do," she said.

"I'm not."

"You are!" she said, "You always have!"

"We were getting somewhere," he protested.

"But I've realised," she said.

"Realised what? What have you realised?"

She paused before saying, "I don't love you."

And he paused before countering, "You do love me."

"I don't," she said, "I've never loved you."

"You can't mean that."

"I can," she said, rising unsteadily to her feet. "I'm sorry. I'm truly sorry. I don't think there was any point in trying after all."

"You can't mean that," he repeated.

"I can," she said, "You see I've had an epiphany."

"Epiphany? I don't even know what that means."

"It means I do want to find love but I can't find it with you. It's time for me to look elsewhere."

"And that's what took you all this time? That's what you decided when you were "taking some air"?"

"Kind of," she said, "I'm truly sorry."

And the man could only watch in confusion as she left the room to sleep elsewhere.

*

"One for Miners and Children"

Every morning about six, Dad would leave the house to go to work down the pit. It was gruelling toil and his lungs coughed and barked regularly, and with much later hindsight I would know that they were done for. Yet every day he'd be there, hail, rain or shine, spring, summer or winter. But it was during the fall that he fell. He was backing his bicycle out of the shed and disappeared down a manhole he didn't know was open.

He was down there for days, nobody could hear his cries for help because he was carried away by sewer subterraliens and taken aboard their vessel and voyaged filthily down and down and down and down to the core of the earth and inter-rogated and tortured by the subterralien government till he begged for mercy because he was just a rank and file worker not a trades unionist. Finally, when they let him go (but con-fiscated his bike) it was me who could hear his cries for help.

"Dad?" I yelled.

"Is that you, Son?" he echoed with much relief.

"Yes, it's me," I said, "What are you doing down a sewer when you should be down a mine?"

"This is no time for smart-arse comments," he said, "get me out of here!"

So I dashed to the garage, found the rope, dangled it down and hauled him up with great human strength for such a young boy of six, back to daylight where he wheezed and writhed in agony. "You OK, Dad?" I asked.

"I think I broke my bloody neck," he said.

"Was it the aliens who broke your neck?" I asked.

"The aliens?" he said, "What the fuck are you talking about?"

119

"I was worried they'd abducted you and taken you to the core of the earth and tortured you."

"Listen, Son," he said, "there were no aliens and I didn't go to the core of the earth. If it hadn't been for some fucking lunatic leaving open the manhole cover, I wouldn't have been down there at all!"

"Sorry, Dad, but that was me," I confessed, "I dreamed there were subterraliens in the sewers under the house and they wanted to take away my dad so I went to investigate."

"You went to what?" said Dad, "Subter fucking aliens?"

"Yes," I said.

"Look, Son," he said, "I've worked down the pit since I was the age of five and never seen a single alien, subter or otherwise. I assure you there are no subterraliens, no aliens of any description, OK?"

"Thanks, Dad," I said, "Then I suppose you better go inside and clean yourself up, you'll be late."

"Son," he said, as we walked back to the house, "what do you want to be when you grow up?"

"A writer," I said.

"A writer huh?" said Dad, "I always knew there was something wrong with you."

"Is there really something wrong with me?" I asked.

"It's just a dream, Son. Just like you dreamed of aliens underneath our house. There's no truth in it."

So then I knew for sure, my dream was just a dream, there were no aliens and in truth I could never be a writer. Then again, and this is the weird thing, Dad never did find his bike.

*

"Shelter"

From the novel "First Boots"

Ryan Brady, homeless for fifteen months, a lost soul who'd found himself in Formby, searched his pockets for the change he'd begged for yesterday and hoped would afford a pint today. Right now, the need for cool sweetness of lager in his mouth and his belly was winning over the need for something less hydraulic despite the bitter cold of the night he'd woken from.

So in a pub called The Grapes he bought a pint of Stella and scanned the busy room for a quiet corner in which to remain anonymous and slake his thirst then eke it out while watching the game. But just as he reached a spare table a man got up from his seat and barged into him, causing his pint to escape his grip and smash to the floor.

"Sorry, mate," said the bloke, automatically. But when he recognised Ryan as the homeless guy often found with his hand out at the railway station he was less apologetic, and simply headed to the gents' with not even an offer of recompense. With that, Ryan headed for the door, knowing his chances of staying put without a drink would be almost nil, being known as he was after begging in the streets for the past few months. He thought about trying but couldn't take the idea of being turfed out for vagrancy – he'd already had daggers from the barmaid who'd come out to brush up the broken pint.

"Wait," said a voice.

Expecting some sort of abuse, verbal or otherwise (people like him could often get a smack on the nose as reward for being homeless) Ryan turned to see the voice belonged to a woman, about his age, brown-haired, attractive.

"Let *me* buy you a drink," she said.

"What?"

"I saw what happened. It was that thug's fault, not yours. He could've at least offered. So let me."

"Are you sure?" asked Ryan, surprised.

"Of course. Sit down and join us."

Taking his seat, Ryan thanked the girl and said his name was Ryan, and she said hers was Rachael and her friend's was Abi, who'd go to the bar for them.

"Stella," said Ryan, gratefully.

Not being used to this kind of charity, Ryan said as much as he thanked Rachael again.

"No need," she said, "Here to watch the game?"

"Yea," he confirmed as Abi set three drinks down, adding that he'd been looking forward to it but because he was homeless there was no guarantee of seeing it, and he once played rugby himself and represented England at schoolboy level.

"Well, now you *can* see the game," she said, "you can see it with us."

"I've got no money," he said, "Only shrapnel."

"We do," said Abi, perhaps a little younger than Rachael, blonde, coy and pretty in a way.

"Cheers," said Ryan.

So they'd chat a little, the two women and Ryan during the game, mostly about the game and the two tries that Jonny May scored, but sometimes about his story and theirs, which was that they were both in HR and big earners but they were currently sharing a house in both their names but one day they'd both be on the property ladder, and that it was a stone's throw from the beach.

Amid these snippets, and loads of crisps, they commented how England were playing well, and how wonderful it must be to represent one's country. Playing it down, Ryan said that was a time when things were going well for him, then after his parents split in angry circumstances he couldn't get on with his step-father so decided to leave home at the age of fifteen. Abi said his story was sad and while agreeing, Rachael added that he was very brave to make that move and it wasn't his fault that things turned bad.

During half time, Rachael said it was her shout and went to the bar. Noting Abi wasn't quite so loquacious, Ryan felt self-conscious and awkward. It was true what Rachael said, his life had turned bad. But he was not like most of them, he didn't accept that he was entirely without hope. Somehow he'd avoided the slippery pavements of the streets he lived on. Sure he'd smoked some weed and done some spice, but had always turned his back on the smackheads and the wasters hooked on barbs and Valium, Lyrica, Pregabalin. He knew guys his age with weeping holes in their legs, who spent every waking day lying in stupor, stinking of piss, dreaming of scoring. He was not like them, because he'd stayed mostly clean. He was a rare exception. These were his thoughts that filled the hundred and twenty yards of silence between Abi and himself, and he was glad when Rachael eventually returned over two journeys with three replenished pints.

"Thanks again," said Ryan.

"Stop saying thanks," said Rachael, firmly.

"Promise I'll never say it again," he said, and they all laughed.

The second half wasn't quite so good, they agreed, dominated by Wales in a hard-fought scrap and not without controversy, but England holding on till the very end. And in that moment amid cheers and toppled bottles, something else happened – Rachael gave Ryan a tight hug and a kiss on the cheek in celebration. In the moment Ryan didn't think much of this, and certainly wouldn't think it was the start of something out of the ordinary for some guy young and on the streets.

But as the pub began to empty following post-match discussion, Rachael and he had one of their own. With Abi nipping to the ladies' and promising another round on her return, Ryan decided then was the moment to broach polite questioning of her kindness.

"Why are you doing this?" he asked, "Being so kind?"

"You promised you wouldn't say thanks," she said.

"I'm not," he said, "I just want to know why. People are never this kind to me."

"Don't you realise we've met before?" said Rachael, smiling a smile he could've fallen in love with.

"What?"

"It's true. We've met before."

"When?"

"Christmas Eve," she said, "In church."

It's true that, on Christmas Eve just gone, Ryan was facing a brittle night on the street and knowing midnight mass was about to happen he'd slipped into the church and was surprised to be ushered to a pew at the front as the place was so packed. It was warmer there and, while not expecting to care for the service itself, it offered an hour or two of comfort. He'd never had much truck with religion; his mum went to a Catholic School in Liverpool but that was as far as it went, and from what he remembered, his dad was deeply suspicious of the man upstairs and in fact most things. But after an hour of sermons and carols, Ryan began to find some peculiar warmth of a different kind – he wouldn't say religious, more spiritual, but anyway it made him cry. At first the tears were perfunctory, dripping occasionally, but gradually they gave way to complete and utter sobbing, so much so that his trackie top was sodden.

"I gave you a tissue," she said, and just then Ryan remembered. Through his sobs he'd felt a hand on his arm and hoped by some miracle it could be his dad, but he turned to see a young woman and her family, and she was offering a tissue to dry his eyes.

"Thanks," he'd said, and she'd said there was no need to thank her.

And as they filed out into the night afterwards he'd wished her a merry Christmas and she'd returned the compliments of the season and asked if he'd somewhere to go to. "No," he'd said, adding that he'd nowhere and nobody to go to.

"To this day I wish I'd invited you to ours for Christmas," she said, "It was just going to be Abi and me."

"That would've been cool," Ryan said, as Abi returned with more drinks. By now the bar was almost empty, just the three of them and a group of stragglers including the bloke who smashed his beer ganging up on the fruit machine and hungrily feeding its belly. Recalling again that night in church, Ryan described how he came to be in the pew, and how he came to realise he was having a spiritual experience.

"I'm not that religious," confessed Rachael, "Dad always insisted we go for mass. That's the only time for me, except for weddings."

"Not much chance of it being your own," Abi bluntly but safely said, given that friendly banter was their currency, and they all laughed.

"It's true I don't have much luck with men," said Rachael, "Anyway most of them are shits."

"Thanks," said Ryan, faux-offended, and they laughed again.

"So what did you actually do at Christmas in the end?" Rachael asked then immediately kicked herself for such a stupidly hollow and cruel question.

"I can't remember," he said, genuinely, adding that the streets are hard and life on them makes nonsense of time, and days like Christmas Day are just the same as any other day.

They had another last drink after that, and chatted pleasantly the three of them, till kicking-out time and Abi said she was ready for home.

As they ventured into the cold February night, happy the game had been won, Ryan said he wouldn't say thanks again but anyway thanks. And as they went to part company, Rachael reached into her bag.

"No," he said, "You've done enough."

"I'm not giving you money," she said, "I'm giving you my number."

"Oh," he said, taking the paper she'd scribbled on with an eyeliner pencil or something.

"You're welcome any time," she said, "Promise you'll phone if you need help?"

"I promise," he said, pocketing the paper and at the same time thinking this would inevitably get lost, and anyway he was between phones. And it was just then when an out of the ordinary and wonderful thing happened, she kissed him on the lips and said, "Actually, come on. We'll get a cab."

When he drifted into The Grapes to eke out a pint and watch the England game, Ryan hadn't expected to be later squeezed into the back of a cab between Rachael and Abi, nor had he expected to be darkening the door of their semi in Formby a stone's throw from the beach.

"It's OK," Rachael said, noting his awkwardness as she stood aside to allow him over the threshold.

"I'm going to bed," said Abi, "Early train to Manchester tomorrow."

"Where her girlfriend lives," explained Rachael.

"Right," said Ryan.

"Go through while I get the kettle on."

Ryan found himself in a large, cosy and carpeted room with plush furniture and welcoming hearth. The teal-coloured walls boasted arty pieces, many of them depicting travel: Cuba, Nassau, Sydney and the ubiquitous New York where workers were astride girders in the sky to eat their lunch, places he'd never been to or ever felt likely to go to.

"Nice," he said, when Rachael returned with a smile. In this light she was not attractive but gorgeous, he thought, fit as, not daring to ask himself how long it was since he'd fucked a woman, not that he was sure a fuck was what this was all about.

"Sit down," she said, "Tea or coffee?"

"Anything."

With a nod she disappeared again into the kitchen. Ryan chose an armchair and sat down, sinking deep, relishing the natural warmth of a radiated house for the first time in God knows, waiting and wondering, exploring the world on the walls, hearing the tinkling tea-making noises off.

"Have you been all these places?" he asked by way of polite conversation and all he could think of as she returned with two steaming mugs.

"God yes," she said, placing the mugs on the coffee table, its glass top shielding compartments containing nick-nacks and further trinkets and mementos of travel.

"Thanks," he said, knowing he shouldn't say that.

"I've been to many places," she said, "Cuba being my favourite. The table's from Ikea."

"Is that the capital?" he joked, and she laughed and said one day she hoped to visit every country in the world but it was a tall order.

"Strange," he said, amid a long pause while they sipped, "Me being here."

"Where have you been sleeping?" she asked, "You don't have to answer if you don't want to."

"By the station. There's a rough bit of ground behind the pub, with like an outbuilding."

"Is that where your stuff is?"

"I haven't got much. Just some clothes and things."

"Don't worry we'll find you something, till morning," she said.

Self-conscious now it was clear he was here for the night, Ryan sought refuge in his drink.

"You must be starving," she said.

"Not really, full of crisps," he answered, and she laughed again, that wonderful sound of a woman laughing, that unbelievable sight of her slender throat tightening as she swished her hair back in mirth.

"Listen," she said, in all seriousness, "you're not sleeping rough tonight, you're staying here."

"It's OK."

"No, I want you to."

"I'll be away tomorrow," he said.

With that she rose and left the room, returning soon after with a dressing gown which she dropped on his lap. "I bought it for my dad when he went into hospital," she said, "he never got chance to wear it."

"Thanks."

"Abi's running you a bath."

127

"You saying I'm dirty?" he quipped, and she laughed again, breaking the sombre moment.

"Not at all."

"I do wash you know," he said, "Service stations, they have showers, facilities."

"Well, tonight you can use our facilities," she said, emphatically.

On the landing, whose thick carpet trod pleasantly towards the sound of running water, he hung back as Abi slipped out of the bathroom.

"'Night," she said, unsmilingly.

"'Night."

Without knowing why, automatically he supposed, Ryan locked the bathroom door behind him before stripping naked. Stepping into the bath was sheer luxury, something he hadn't experienced since, he recalled, living with his Auntie Doreen and her wanker of a boyfriend the first few nights after leaving home. He sank into its foamy depths and looked around the bathroom, clad entirely in tile, nothing on the walls but shelving containing various creams, soaps, scented candles and incense. The only adornment was a postcard stuck to the back of the door bearing a poem: *If no air-freshener in the loo, slip out quiet so nobody knows it was you.* Ryan read this over about four times, trying to memorise it and for some inexplicable reason assuming it'd been stuck there by Abi not Rachael. Thinking back, he got the impression Abi wasn't happy about him being here – she'd said hardly a word in the cab and when Rachael left the living room earlier he'd heard muffled voices that didn't altogether sound agreeable.

Whatever, he was here now, having a hot foamy bath run by Abi, with possible reluctance, feeling the cleanest he'd felt for ages and, he couldn't help noticing, the hardest, his member periscoping out of the depths and staring him in the eye as if to say, "Hello? What have we here?"

He thought about that – what indeed had he here? Abi didn't seem too enamoured for obvious reasons but what about Rachael? Why was she taking him in like this? She hardly knew him, bar offering him a tissue in church on

Christmas Eve. He'd been in weird and surprising situations before, nobody living on the streets for ages hadn't; he'd given a bloke a hand job behind Home Bargains for twenty quid, he'd been taken for a ride by a homeless girl in Tranmere who he thought was going to shag him but was only after a few quid to buy some spice, he'd been invited to move in with a bloke with one leg who had a fetish for licking toes… But this? What *did* we have here? Was it sex? Some weird fetish? Rachael seemed pretty straight but you never know, looks deceive and you don't live on the street without cross-referencing, watching your back. Because what would a beautiful, tall, slim brunette want with a no-mark like him? He'd still got his looks, but… He towelled himself dry and put on the dressing gown she'd given him. *Dead man's dressing gown*, he thought, and left the room.

When he padded downstairs, somehow wishing his cock would behave and somehow wishing it wouldn't, he found Rachael leaving the kitchen having taken the mugs away.

"That better?" she asked.

"Feels great."

"Obviously," she said, with a look. "Shall we go up?"

"You sure?" he said.

"Look I won't be cruel," she said, "We're not going to fuck, I just want you in with me. If that's a problem, there's a spare room."

"It's not a problem," he said, thinking otherwise, and she led the way, saying they'd have to be quiet because of Abi and her early start.

Rachael's bedroom was tastefully furnished, like every other room he'd seen in the house thus far. The walls were neutral and this time pictureless but family photographs stood neat and smiling on every available surface. "Get into bed," she whispered, "while I do my ablutions."

As she left the room, Ryan did as he was told, loving the soft cool touch of the duvet, the first time he'd felt a duvet in God knew how long. After a few moments, Rachael returned, switched off the light and padded over to the bed, which bounced as she sat to remove her earrings and bangles. He heard them clatter onto the bedside cabinet, then felt her slip into the bed beside him.

"You sure you're all right with this?" she said.

"Sure," he said, "but only if you are."

"Spoon me," she said, turning foetal.

Ryan did as he was told, knowing his cock would be twitching and knowing she'd be feeling it in the small of her back.

"I don't want to be cruel but let's just talk," she said, and added that this was the first time she'd slept with a bloke for months. There was no agenda here, except her need to be held at last.

And so he did, he held her and talked. He told her more about how he finished up on the streets after walking out on his mum and step-dad, how at first he went to his auntie Doreen's but couldn't stand her boyfriend with whom it came to blows and he had to move on. She told him about her job and her plans to travel the world, and her plans to one day be on the property ladder in her own right, and how her mum was in a nursing home and she sees her regularly but she only knows her sometimes, other times she's away with the fairies, and how her dad died three months ago and it broke her heart because she loved him, and how painful it was to decide not to take her mother, his wife for over thirty years, to the funeral. She asked if he'd ever had a girlfriend and he said he was once in love but she fucked his best mate and there'd been nobody serious since. He asked if she'd ever had a boyfriend and she said several but most of them were tossers. She hoped one day she'd get married and have kids but it doesn't look likely, Abi was right.

He began to recount childhood memories; his first pair of boots his dad bought him when he was picked for the school team, how they'd go to the park and his dad would show him tricks with the ball, how to catch it properly and how to be strong in the scrum and how to kick. "Put your laces through it!" he'd say. How his dad would come and watch him play for the school in the rain, and when he took him to Twickenham for the first time and he was filled with awe. And then when he got picked for England and his dad gave him £500 as a present but that was the last time he saw him…

He realised Rachael was asleep – he could hear the changing of her breath – but he stayed like that, spooning her and holding her, feeling the rise and fall of her breast and hearing the sibilant snore of slumber. He thought back to that childhood, and the question he'd asked a million times that never got answered, about why his dad upped and went. He thought about the times they were happy, and they truly were, Christmases and things when he always got what he wanted. Scalextrics, Playstation, Wii Sports. Yet in the depths of memory he'd perhaps been drowning there were words and slamming doors, muffled arguments in the bedroom carried over. What sounded like blows. His dad saying life was only a series of disappointments and lies, like the advert that showed Scalextrics performing miracles when reality was it forever left the track, a waste of fucking money. No more fucking disappointments. And then he must have slept.

In the morning he woke alone, blinking at the day and wondering for a minute where the fuck he was. But soon the door opened and Rachael entered, fully-dressed for work in a sharp suit and fetching with her a cup of tea and sweet smell of perfume.

"Wakey, wakey," she said, "I've brought you a drink."

"Thanks," he said, struggling up, trying to make some sense of things.

He watched as she sat at her dressing table, tied up her hair and looked in the mirror to do her lipstick and said, "Lovely story by the way."

"What?"

"About your dad. You must miss him terribly. I miss mine."

"I thought you were asleep."

"I still heard," she said, "So what are you going to do today?"

"Dunno," he said, "What about you?" he added, as if for all the world they were together and this was the norm when usually he'd be alone and wondering where was the next meal.

"Work I'm afraid," she said, "but don't feel you have to get up. Abi's already left."

"But what should I do when you've gone?"

"Have breakfast first you must be starving," she said, "then if you go out just close the door behind you it'll be OK."

Still trying to take all this in, Ryan paused, before saying, "I can't believe you trust me. Nobody trusts people like me."

"Well I do," she said. "Look, I know last night was weird, and you won't be here when I get back. But you're a nice guy. And I needed this too. Right?"

"Right," he said, as she put the finishing touches to herself before grabbing her handbag and keys.

"That's me," she said, "Now have something to eat and take care."

With that, she gave him a peck on the cheek and was gone.

From the dimly daylit bedroom Ryan heard the front door close and soon after a car engine start up as he sipped his tea. Then, he got up, shook off the dead man's dressing gown before fishing his clothes from the bathroom. Downstairs he helped himself to breakfast, just a bowl of cornflakes, before heading for the front door. But just as he was about to leave, he spotted a note on the console table in the hall, atop a pile of money:

Take this, it said, *Buy some food, find your dad.*
Good luck, Rachael
ps. we don't say thanks but anyway thanks x

Rhyme or reason for any of this escaping him, Ryan counted the notes, one hundred pounds, then left the premises, dutifully closing the door and making sure it was locked.

"Day Return to Cocoa Yard"

"Are you ready?" said Anna to her dad, having helped slip him into his jacket, the linen one her mother had chosen because the weather was warm.

"Ready," he said.

"Is your back better now?"

"Better now."

They were going to meet Harry's friends in a pub called The Barrel in the town of Marlin, where he'd been a regular for thirty years.

Ever since Harry's health had begun to deteriorate, they'd been doing this every week and sometimes he'd remember it and sometimes not.

"Come on then," said Harry's wife Mary, "there might be a football match for you to watch."

"Football match," said Harry.

Mary smiled at Anna and she smiled back. It was always nice to see Dad offering some sort of conversation and she was grateful at least for that.

*

At the same time as the three of them were leaving Mary and Harry's house, a traveller called Terry Walker who preferred to be called Walker was heading down the high street of Marlin and saw that a pub called The Barrel was showing football. He opened the door and chose the lounge side, where there was just a handful of 3 o'clockers taking varnish off the bar. One week previous, Walker had had a bet – a 300/1 shot that there wouldn't be a single goalless draw in the entire World Cup competition. He'd put down a hundred quid and so far all was rosy to pick up thirty grand, which would fund his travels for a good while longer. And so there he was, nursing a pint of heavy and ready for France v Denmark, both of whom had qualified but would hopefully go for gold and top the group, meaning of course there would be goals

Walker was thirty-six, a loner now who liked to be alone, who got his kicks in the bookies', so many kicks that he lost his woman and friends in that order. Ten years ago he was living with Pip, they were happy or at least he was, planning to get married and have kids. But that never happened because it was his gambling that was the issue. She'd lived with it for years in which he liked to call it a hobby while she preferred the term addiction. And when he lost his wages on poker, indulging his hobby with the rent going begging, she could live with his addiction no more.

And yes, Walker had friends once; Toby, Yoda, Flick and Pogo, who'd hog the games tables of Workingmen's Clubs back home, betting on everything, poker, bastard brag, pontoon, dominoes, the gender of the next person to walk in the door... He was the ringleader, the master, the kingpin on a winning streak, at least till the day he bet away his friends as well when one of them welshed and blows were traded. If he were a psychologist, he'd study this downward spiral and conclude it was deliberate, because once he'd lost his girlfriend and his friends and had his own company and travel, he was happy at last. Happy to never work again, just live hand to mouth, odd-jobbing and seeing the world, not officially existing but being. Happy that was until the French and the Danes fucked his bet by drawing nil-nil in the dourest game of the entire tournament.

Walker hated the French. Ever since he rode a night bus from Paris to Lyon and was joined on the back seat by three Paris skins. Thinking he was English they began to taunt him, throwing Saxonisms his way like fuck off and piss off, and the English are scum. Even when he told them he was Scottish they persisted, saying they hated everything British. Fair enough, he'd said, and when the bus hit Macon he got off and they did too, and scrapped with him on the station platform till he was lying half dead.

"The most boring game of the whole tournament that," said one of the men at the bar going by the name of Gordon, Gord to his friends, who agreed. "Fucking shite," said a bloke called Hen. "I don't know why you bovvered watching it," pronounced the barmaid called Ange and they concurred profusely, like they concurred profusely with everything she pronounced on account of her pronounced cleavage.

Walker concurred too but didn't say as much, in fact he said nothing, he just sat wetting his belly with his newspaper in front of him, ruing the thirty grand unwon and thinking he'd maybe have a monkey on the English reaching the Final. Call it consolation.

Listening to the witty or banal conversation of the now five o'clock dregs, he smiled to himself.

"It'll be raucous in here on Fursday," said Ange, of the forthcoming game against the Belgians, "Fank Christ I'm on me holidays."

"*We're all going on a Summer Holiday,*" sang Gord, as close as he could manage to Cliff, and whose thing it was to set every desultory pontification to music, and whose thing it was to delude himself that the much younger Ange could be won over with his crooning.

"Belgium are a good side," said Hen, "we'll soon see how good England are."

"We've played nobody so far," agreed a bloke named Daz.

"You can only beat what's in front of you," Jigger philosophised.

"Yea fucking Panama," countered Daz, his glass always half-broken.

"If anybody can beat us it's the Belgians with de Bruyne in the side," agreed Hen, "I'll have you any money they show us how it's done."

"*Money Money Money,*" sang Gord, jangling his trouser pocket.

Walker supped his third pint of heavy and pondered all this – personally he backed England to win on Thursday and would *definitely* have a punt on them reaching the final, just to spite Daz, who he didn't know but didn't like. He loathed negative attitudes, he preferred to believe, even when staring down the barrel of defeat. Surely if you're English you back your team? Or maybe Daz wasn't in fact English? He wouldn't ask, because he didn't like him and didn't care – he seemed to be one of them know-all Yorkshiremen who argue just to pass the time, a commodity they all obviously had too much of in their meaningless existence.

"How you getting to the airport, sweetheart?" Hen asked Ange.

"Bus to Leeds Bradford," she said.

"*Oh the wheels on the bus go round and round*," sang Gord.

"Oh Christ," said Jigger.

"Everyfin you say he puts to sodding music," said Ange, with the air of someone desperate to get on the plane.

"*The hills are alive…*," sang Gord out of light-hearted and delusional defiance.

"Where are you going again?" Daz asked Ange.

"Andalucia," said Ange, and had he known where Andalucia was, Gord would've sung *Y viva Espana*. But he didn't, so he didn't, and everybody was glad of his geographical ignorance.

"Right, I'm off home or she'll be coming at me with her rolling pin," said Hen after a brief lull, and promptly ordered another pint.

"I'll have one with you," said Daz, who then began an anecdote about the trouble he'd had with his car – something about the mechanic telling him it was the starter motor but he knew best of course. But nobody was really listening. In fact, they were glad of three more people coming in and serving a diversion.

"Hello, Harry!" exclaimed Ange.

"Here he is!" said Hen.

"Hello," said Mary, "Go and sit down love and I'll get you a drink."

While Mary went to the bar, Anna escorted him to a chair near Walker.

"Sit there, Dad," she said, "mum's getting you a drink."

"How is he?" Jigger asked Mary.

"Still the same," she said, "sometimes he knows us sometimes he doesn't."

"It's a bugger of a thing," Daz diagnosed, and this time nobody could disagree, not least Mary who, while Walker didn't know it yet, had lived with this for years now and was in all honesty at her wits' end but would never show it. She couldn't. She wouldn't.

Walker looked at Harry, who struggled to his feet and looked back at him with eyes that said I wonder if I know you. "Hello," he said, feeling for some reason like he for once ought to make conversation.

"Sorry," said Anna, "sit down, Dad, let the gentleman read his paper."

"Hello," said Harry.

"Hello," Walker said back.

"Is it time for your tablet, Dad?" Anna asked, and explained to Walker that he'd been complaining of a bad back.

By this time Mary had finished the small-talk with the barflies and was joining her daughter and husband with three drinks, one of which ferried by helpful Hen because she couldn't carry them all.

"Thanks, Hen," said Mary.

"How are you, Harry?" asked Hen.

"You remember Hen," said Mary, "It's Hen, off the buses."

"Hen," said Harry, more by rote than familiarity.

"He's grumbling about his back," Anna told her mum.

"I'll give him a tablet," she said, zipping open her handbag.

"Cheers, Dad," said Anna.

"Hen," said Harry, this time with recognition, "Off the buses."

"That's me, Harry," said Hen, "Those were the days eh?"

As Mary popped a blister pack, Walker wondered if this were a real tablet or placebo and wanted to ask but didn't. Somehow reading his mind, Anna struck up a conversation, telling him they saw the first signs about five years ago when her dad was forced to retire from the buses which he'd driven for thirty-five years. He was well-known for being cheerful, giving the time of day to man, woman and child. Always a smile and a chat, always a joke or a firm but well-meant reproach when schoolkids were cheeky. A strong man, a kind man and one who'd be joined at the bar by all and sundry knowing they'd be in for good company. The company for whom he worked rewarded his thirty-five year service with a clock and a healthy redundancy which they'd put by for when he eventually went into a home because they couldn't cope. For the first time in ages Walker felt bound by conversation.

"Thirty-five years," he said, admiringly.

"A long time," mused Mary, a small woman with dark hair who was once a looker but was now lined like a sawn-off branch showing her years.

"Real grafter my dad," said Anna, who was her father's daughter according to her features. She was good-looking, he thought, but beginning to show the dark rings of a weary carer.

"Prided himself on his driving," said Mary, "Didn't you, Harry? Pride yourself on your driving?"

"My back," he muttered.

"He's hard work now," said Anna, if she were brutally honest.

"But we love him," Mary said in peroration.

"Can I get you another drink?" asked Walker, thinking to himself it was a long time since he'd said those words on account of spending most of his days with only himself for company to buy for.

"No thanks," Anna said, "very kind of you though."

At the bar, Walker asked Ange for another pint of heavy and she duly obliged while trying to explain to Gord where on the map was Andalucia.

"Just tell him it's in fucking Spain," said Daz.

"Does he even know where fucking Spain is?" she said.

"Of course, I know where fucking Spain is," said Gord.

"Somewhere near China innit?" said Hen.

"You're taking the piss now," said Gord.

"Spain could win it actually," said Jigger, seemingly eager to change tack to the World Cup.

"*Y viva Espana*," Gord sang, cottoning on at last.

"How are you getting to the airport you say?" Hen asked Ange.

"Bus!" she cried for the umpteenth time.

"*The wheels on the bus go round and round,*" sang Gord.

When Walker returned with his pint to his seat, Anna and Mary had a hand apiece of Harry, who he noticed was shedding a quiet tear.

"Is he all right?" Walker asked, and they said nothing, just silently weeping themselves to see a strong man weakened. Until finally Anna said, "Are you all right, Dad?" And he looked up at her and said, "Day Return to Cocoa Yard please."

"I know, Dad," she said.

"It sounds like a nice place," said Walker, wondering to himself if this held some special memory between the man and his wife and his daughter.

And it was at that moment when the old man began to quietly sing...

"The wheels on the bus go round and round
Round and round
Round and round
The wheels on the bus go round and round..."

and Anna and Mary and Walker and everybody joined in with "*All day long.*" And as the men at the bar and even Walker gave Harry a clap, Mary wept openly and said to Harry, "You do know I love you don't you?"

And he said, "I love you too Mary. And I love you too Anna."

When Walker left the pub he found that he himself was in tears. To think of that poor old man. Thirty-five years' graft, strong-armed at the wheel, always a smile and a joke and a firm but well-meant reproach for cheeky schoolkids, pillar of the community, company at the bar. A teller of tales, a font of knowledge not just geographical, a proud man travelled who knew things about the world, who knew where on the map was Andalucia. Who'd never harmed a soul. A hardworking man who was now hard work, destined for a home with the lingering smell of piss.

And he thought to himself, *Were they really dregs, these people? Was their conversation so banal and meaningless, or did it just make their wheels go round?* They were simple people the same as the simple people he'd met in many towns on his travels and what was so wrong with that? What did it matter? Winning thirty grand or unwinning thirty grand, if England made the final or not, what did that, or anything, really matter?

Heading back to the town square, he bought a limp sandwich from a pound bakery and sat near the cenotaph to ponder where he'd travel to next. Amid the sorrow at seeing such a strong, hardworking man with a good brain wasting, he couldn't help feeling selfishly irritated. He'd always been the optimist, hated negativity, but he'd been made to feel far from positive about life itself. So what *did* it matter? What did anything matter? What the fuck was it all about? True he'd been nagged by the dog all his adult life, or at least since Pip slammed out on him, and the dog is by definition pessimistic, and true that he'd battled with his gambling addiction. But he'd always chosen to view this as a hobby, something good, a positive, because with betting there was hope. Yet meeting Harry had left him questioning that very thing – is winning or losing and the journey to either so important? And what really was everybody hoping *for?* he asked himself as he threw the crust of his limp sandwich to the pigeons gambling on a meal at his feet, spinning and clockworking like famished avian robots.

"I'd hoped you hadn't gone far," a voice said, just as he was about to walk away into the warm night and head towards where he'd parked his campervan near a retail park on the edge of this town called Marlin.

"Hello," he said.

"I just wanted to thank you."

"Thank me? Why?"

"The way you spoke to my dad. You didn't know him yet you seemed to give him life. Mum said I should go after you."

"But why?"

"Thing is," she said, "May I sit down? It's so hot."

Walker slid his rucksack along the seat and she sat and said, "I can't be long, he needs me."

"You do a brilliant job," he said, "I could see it's hard."

"You mean I look tired," she said, smiling, and suddenly he saw the dark rings around her eyes dissipate and her beauty for what it was before.

"All I'm saying is it must take its toll at times," he said.

"I hate it," she said, "it brings me out in eczema. That's why I cover up. I can't tan like you. I don't even know why I said that." He hadn't noticed this in the pub, but now saw how pale was her skin compared to his, and how she was wearing more clothing than many in such heat.

"It's a sad thing and I'm sure it's a lot of stress to go through what you're going through with your dad," he said.

"Sometimes I wish he were dead," she said, "that must sound cruel."

"Not really. You mean an end to suffering." With that she somberly nodded, and Walker found himself explaining how it'd made *him* feel – the way it made him question life, which now seemed as meaningless and arbitrary as that of the pigeons still at his feet, tossing the crust in the air to bounce and create some throat-sized chunks.

"Who said anything about pigeons?" she asked, again with the smile that made her face.

"Doesn't matter," he said, smiling back.

"Well, anyway Mum and I talked. She said she could see a spark in me, when I talked to you. Sorry if this sounds stalkerish but she said I needed some fun, and I should go after you."

"What for?" Walker asked, wondering and liking and nervous about where this was going.

"Fun I guess," she said.

"Some would say I'm not much fun," he said.

"You mean your girlfriend? Wife?"

"I'm single," he said, "my girlfriend walked out on me years ago. Been on my own ever since. Just me and my rucksack."

"Are you an explorer?"

"I prefer experientialist. Just me and my campervan and my rucksack and my experiences."

"Well, *that's* fun," she said, "what else do you do for experience?"

"I like a bet," he said, "Gambling. Horses, football, where I'll go next… That's why she walked out on our relationship."

"So where *will* you go next?"

"That's what I mean, I never know till I get there. Or when the money runs out, or the van claps out."

"You won't stay long in this dump I would imagine."

"Don't you like it?"

"Dead," she said, "Nothing ever happens. I don't even know why the bloody pigeons insist on staying."

"So what do *you* do for experiences in this dead town?" he asked.

"I'm single too if that's what you mean."

"It wasn't but anyway."

"I *was* married. Childhood sweethearts, thought the world of him, he *was* my world and yet…"

"Yet?"

"Tony always wanted kids," she said, looking across the square beyond the pound bakery and into the distance of painful memory, "but I didn't. I loved him madly but couldn't see myself having kids while living in this hole. I'd've wanted more for them than growing up here. Tony said we should move away then, but his job was here and so was mine. Then with what was happening to Dad. He couldn't handle that. I understand why but I resented him for not caring enough. So in hindsight I realise that was the beginning of the end. Two years later we were divorced."

"So how long ago was this?"

"A year ago."

"And since?"

She didn't reply to that because she couldn't, because she was crying, so Walker just let the moment linger, wondering whether to touch her arm, give her a tissue or something.

"Thanks," she said, taking the tissue, "you must think I'm bonkers."

"I don't think you're bonkers at all," he summarised.

"I can't believe I'm telling you all this."

"I can't believe I told you I like to gamble. Can't say I'm proud of it."

"I ought to get back to dad," she said.

"Of course."

And then she paused, looked him in the eye and said, "I wonder, and feel free to tell me to bog off, but will you have dinner with me before you move on to wherever it is you find yourself next?"

"I'm not sure I find myself wherever I go," he said, and they both laughed.

*

She'd been scared when asking Walker out to dinner with its encoded offer of sex. She'd even provided a disclaimer for fear of rejection. But he'd accepted and now, having tidied her two-up-two-down in the town called Marlin that she thought was dead, she was checking herself in the mirror with nervous excitement. This would mean so much to her, be-cause it would be the first time she'd had a date, if it were to be deemed so, since Tony when he plucked up the courage to ask her out all those years ago. She'd actually seen her ex-husband that morning, not knowing at the time that seeing him

143

would be a kind of revelation, a portentous glimpse of a past existence and future life. On seeing him she'd decided without prejudice that he was not a well man. Once, he was a strong, broad-shouldered, even hunky guy, but now he seemed small and wasted in the chinos he always wore, the chinos she'd bought for him from George on the retail park some five years ago.

"Go after him," her mum had said of the interesting stranger in the pub, who'd given her father life with some kind words and the offer of a drink, and some polite and refreshing conversation for Anna. And she'd thought twice, but there was another voice telling her to go after him besides the one of her mother, and that voice was the one in her head that had been telling her what she needed since Tony finally closed the door on their marriage. And so she did go after him, and she did find him in the dead square, feeding half-dead pigeons with the crust of his limp sandwich from the pound bakery, looking travelled, tanned and fascinating in his shorts, hiking-boots, bohemian top and hat – every inch the man the inner voice was telling her had seen life and *lived* it.

"But have *you* lived it?" she asked the woman staring back at her from the mirror. The answer was that since Tony left, no. What had she got when he had gone? A little cottage she loved, that's true, which would always be hers as one day would the house belonging to her parents since she was the only child; a clerical job that paid OK but not much of a social life and anyway not much time for that since Dad got ill; a non-existent sexlife; and this fucking eczema she was born with and had carried for the rest of her days – behind her ears and neck, her shoulders, elbows, behind her knees and, worst of all, between her thighs where Betnovate had been applied with desperate thickness.

"You're depressed," said her mum on more than one occasion; in fact, several, "you should see the doctor."

But Anna had resisted. Ever since she was a child she'd suffered and having taken a million pills and smeared a thousand creams with no results, she'd grown a deep mistrust of medics and medication of any kind. So if she did see the doctor what would he do? Tell her to pop some pill or other, give it three weeks and if there's no change come back and we'll put you on something else to pop. The pharmaceutical industry, after all, needed the money. One thing was sure to Anna, she didn't want pills to pop, she needed a life to live, and tonight she was going to find one, or at least just a bit of one amid the grim circumstances she'd found herself in.

In the mirror she looked OK, she thought, having decided to wear her hair down. Should've had the roots done but too late for that now. Just some eyeliner, she'd never needed too much make-up, that was one thing in her favour, she was naturally, at least in her view, good-looking, not pretty, not beautiful, good-looking. And of course just a bit of lippy to set things off and smile at this interesting man about her age, handsome, travelled, erudite and quite by chance sitting in The Barrel with his newspaper, and where they'd taken Dad to see his old friends Gordon, Hen, Daz and Jigger.

"Did you find me OK?" she asked that man who stood on the threshold clutching a bottle of Sauvignon.

"Evidently," he replied with a smile.

"Only I was worried my directions were vague. Or that you wouldn't come at all."

"I'm a traveller," he said, "I sometimes don't know where somewhere is but always know it when I get there."

"Come in," she said, not knowing whether his reply was clever or indeed made sense. "Dinner won't be long I hope you like lasagne, threw it together I'm afraid I didn't have much time, I never get much of that you see, after work I go and see to Mum and Dad and everything, in fact it's shop bought, I'd planned to pass it off as my own creation but oh my God I'm waffling aren't I, please sit down."

"A bit," he said, knowing this was borne out of nerves and liking her all the more for it because actually he was a bit shaky himself.

Having put his bottle in the fridge for later and opened the cheaper version she'd grabbed from Morrison's with the lasagne, she joined him at the table she'd carefully prepped.

"It's a lovely home," he said, and she was proud but said it's nothing much but she has it how she likes it. "Why is it called Chocolate Cottage?"

"Oh that? Because it's near to Cocoa Yard. But it's more of a joke, a homage to Dad and the story he once invented for me."

"Interesting. You must tell it me, I'd like to hear it," he said, frankly.

"I'd be a bag of nerves," she said, as they began to eat, "I'm already a bit nervous to be honest with you."

"Me too," he reassured, "it's kind of you to go to all this trouble, for a man you don't even know. I was *very* surprised to get the invitation to dinner."

"I surprised myself!" she laughed, "But I'm glad."

"I'm glad your mum told you to come and find me," he said, and she smiled that smile he'd liked with the teeth.

So with every forkful of food, complimented accordingly, there came chunks of small-talk and increasing confidence on both sides to free things up and widen the subject matter. She asked him about his travels and he documented with wit and wisdom his experiences in such exotic places some of which she'd never even heard of, he asked her about her job and she managed to speak at length about it and—shock, shock horror —even make it sound interesting…and then he asked about her father, about whom she could also speak at length.

"I'm really a daddy's girl I suppose," she said, "ever since I remember, he was my favourite. Because he was the one who'd read me bedtime stories, he'd teach me things. I remember when I was about seven and I'd hurt my knee and he said he'd make it go away and I asked if you could make *anything* go away even people, even the past, and he told me about the Grandfather Paradox, the theory of *changing* the past. I'll never forget that, I never forget a lot of things we talked about and we talked about a lot of things, always did. The other week we laughed, because after thirty-five years I finally confessed I was embarrassed at school because my dad was only a bus driver. But then I qualified it, saying he could've been so much more because he *was* so much more,

146

he could've been a teacher, professor even, and he said he *was* a professor, professor of the buses, "the omnipotent, omniscient omnibus driver!" Yea we talked and laughed like we always did, like we sometimes still do… When he knows who I am."

"Who says he *ever* knew you?"

"What?"

"Who really knows anyone is what I mean. Do we know *ourselves*?"

"That's true," she said, "I don't know myself sometimes," then added with a laugh that they were getting a bit deep but it was true what he said, she *didn't* know herself, she certainly didn't know herself earlier when she was so forward and inviting him to dinner.

"I like forward," he concluded, and that was the start of it.

*

"That was nice," said Anna, as they lay on her bed afterwards.

"Nice?" Walker said.

"I know, that was a stupid thing to say. You made me see colours if you know what I mean."

Walker didn't know what she meant but took it as a compliment and said nothing. Tied together with her by the post-coital chord, he could now see the eczema on her bloated flesh, like a map of itchy countries she used to be self-conscious of but now was liberated from, or so it seemed. It was ages since he'd slept with a woman, he'd spent so much time on his own and travelling that sometimes he'd wondered if he'd ever sleep with a woman again. He certainly didn't expect to tonight, with a woman he'd only met that afternoon while drinking with the five o'clockers of The Barrel in some town called Marlin that she called dead.

"I know I said I wanted casual sex," she said, "but I think it'll be more than that. Causal not casual, if you know what I mean."

"Yea I know what you mean," Walker said, again not really knowing what she meant. Privately he feared this was getting deep and she might want to see him again, so wondered if he should add that he was moving on tomorrow, but decided it'd be impolite in the circumstances so added only silence.

"I want to explore every inch of you," he'd said as they lay naked. Then, she'd felt reassured when he was kissing and licking up her leg and remaining for some time on her thigh before everything else that happened and she didn't need to climax because she didn't want it to end. Then afterwards they'd talked a little while and she'd told him she'd seen colours, and he'd said he'd known what she meant when he hadn't, and she'd explained when she's down she usually sees grey, but those colours she saw just then on the bed were bright, and the eczema was something she'd been freed of in a way. And finally, they'd slept.

To Anna it hadn't mattered when out of politeness he stopped himself from saying he'd be moving on. And it didn't matter next morning when, amid his awkwardness she said it's fine, she knows he's an explorer, 'an experientialist'... What mattered most, she'd ponder when he'd gone, was that she'd taken control. The scared woman who didn't know herself had made this happen; after work that day she'd go and visit Mum and Dad as always; she'd tell her mum what happened after she'd stalked the man with his newspaper in the pub, and above all else what it really meant. It wasn't casual sex it was causal sex. The girl who'd been embarrassed at school because her father was just a bus driver had become the woman who took control, said no to her moods and to hell with the eczema. All was so clear and certain to Anna now, except when to tell her mum what her dad had said, right at the beginning of his illness, and so seriously, and put in writing with the precision of a bus timetable, about wanting to end his life.

*

148

After leaving Anna's two-up-two-down the morning after, Walker had planned to move on. But something in the traveller had changed, again he wasn't sure exactly when, or even why, but something made him decide instead of leaving for the next town to stay in this one, the one where Anna lived, the one she said was dead with half-dead pigeons. The one where Anna lived. Was he hoping to see her again? Was he drawn in some way to the town's peace and serenity, resting as it was, waiting for someone or something to breathe life into it again? The town that was like many across the country, seemingly waiting for a World Cup run to kick it into life. Or was it Anna? Sex notwithstanding it had been a pleasant evening, the first one in such a long time he'd spent with another person, with a woman, the first one in even longer that finished up in bed. So sex, after all, was not notwithstanding. Perhaps, he wondered, there'd been life breathed back into *him*. Like the town itself, like the thousands of men, women and children looking to England's progress in the World Cup as some sort of saviour, he was looking for someone or something too. It made no difference that he'd got two hundred quid on England beating Sweden, and a further three on them going all the way. It made no odds that he found himself remaining, planning to join the hordes to watch the next game in the pub where they met. Yes, what was really happening was that he was hoping for another glimpse of Anna. That was what he finally decided.

After he left her two-up-two-down the morning after, Anna decided that actually she'd phone in sick. It was something she'd never done in ten years with the company she worked for and she wanted to know why. She wasn't sick at all, she was very well, in fact she was more than that, she was good; for the first time in ages, sex notwithstanding, she was feeling alive. It had been a very pleasant evening, the conversation, the laughter, what Walker did for her in bed. So sex, after all, was not notwithstanding; it was outstanding. Thus feeling alive, she phoned in sick, stayed unshowered and not entirely dressed and spent the day in bed, doing little, thinking a lot and masturbating a lot more. Thinking of Walker and his exotic tales of travel, thinking did she make the right choice of meal that remained half-eaten? Did they drink her bottle of plonk too quickly before moving on to his more expensive Sauvignon? Was the loss of inhibition and self-conciousness about her body and its fucking eczema down to alcohol or the interesting stranger who'd crashed into her life? She'd never see him again of course, he'd made that clear in his minimal way, he was moving on, he was a traveller and experientialist, life for him a fascinating action-packed or so it appeared string of this and that and whatevers. A traveller who sometimes doesn't know the somewhere he's going to but always knows it when he's there. That's what he said or something like that and what she tried to make sense of. And she was also thinking of what her dad had said about dying and what she was going to do about it. When to tell her mum? She'd gathered and printed research off the internet. Dignitas. Dying with dignity. The right to die. The arguments for and against. Whether one should have the right to leave or remain. The moral discussions, the principle dilemmas. What side would Mum fall down on when she finally found the courage to tell her that Dad's right to live or die was his? Would it be right to keep him alive when he wanted not to be left to die an undignified death? Was it selfish to let him choose or was it selfish of *him* to choose?

The morning after the morning after that, she didn't phone in sick but carried into work this cocktail of questions, this potent mix of emotions. Colleagues saw that something had changed in her but didn't know what and didn't ask because it was private and after all, they knew she was prone to mood swings. But Anna also knew something had changed. Walking home through the dead town she saw the bunting on the pubs, the flag of St George proudly waving back at anyone who looked, she felt the shift in atmosphere, the expectant nationalistic, patriotic and jingoistic buzz that had been lost to the town over the past ten years since factories had shut. Dad had wanted to watch the next game, against Sweden, in the pub with his friends Hen, Jigger, Gord and Daz, and wanted her and Mum to join him. Sadly not in the pub where she met the fascinating stranger, another one that'd been brought back to life, chosen for its multiple screens. It was a blow because she wanted to glimpse that man again, just on the off-chance he'd stayed, but it was what she'd do, for Dad. And then the morning after that she'd phone in sick again, arrange for Dad to go to the day centre and sit her mum down. To tell her what Dad had said. Show her the letter he'd handwritten and signed and dated with the precision of a bus timetable. And tell her that she wanted to spend her dad's redundancy on a trip to Switzerland. That was what she finally decided.

*

"I can see a change in you," said Mary to Anna.

"Really?"

"Yes. Your face is back but then it isn't."

It was a strange thing to say, Anna thought, or a strange way to put it, but she knew her mum was right; that morning the woman who looked back from the mirror was a different woman, one whose eyes were no longer ringed, whose smile was not painted. They were in a pub called the White Horse in Cocoa Yard or strictly-speaking its carpark on which a marquee had been hastily erected for the World Cup Quarter Final between Sweden and England. The brewery's expense in their eyes was justified – the town and its pubs and its people had journeyed from doubt before the tournament to apathy in its group stage to the excitement of possibility and hope, and this now, this pub now like all the rest, had been turned into an open-air theatre where sleeping wasn't an option as dreams were real. Anna's dad, Harry, had been parked in a chair with his friends Gord, Hen, Daz and Jigger, Anna and her mum on the table behind, all with adequate views of the big screen.

"My face is back but then it isn't? I don't understand."

"Is there something you want to tell me?" said her mum.

Anna didn't usually talk to her mum about such things as sex, she didn't talk about much at all to her mum and never had. She'd always talked to Dad, the man who would tuck her up at night and read bedtime stories and tell her about the Granfather Paradox and lots of other things too. But here, in a setting that could be viewed unusual, incongruous even inappropriate, she was talking to her mum about sex, and sex with the interesting stranger who'd walked into her life and she'd been told and had felt compelled to go after. She didn't really expect her mum to understand the notion of *casual* sex but told her anyway and simplified it thus, that it was simply deep and meaningful, and though she'd never see the man again her one night stand would live with her for ever. Because he'd changed things, he'd made her come alive. And she even found herself telling her mum she'd seen Tony that morning and thought he looked like a man not well, and funny that it was a kind of epiphany and when she asked the stranger to dinner there was an undercurrent of more on the menu. And profound the way he made love to her the way she never knew before; whereas she'd just let Tony do his thing to her, this man did things *with* her, and it felt like love even though it wasn't and could never be perhaps. And that the fucking eczema although she didn't use that 'F' word to her mother, was an itch forgotten.

"Well," said her mum, more to curtail matters than to prolong them.

"Well what?" said Anna, sensing and not caring that a reproach was on its way.

"I don't understand all of what you said but I could see a change in you, I could see there was something on your mind. Anyway, perhaps you will see him again, perhaps he won't go away."

"Perhaps. But what did you mean by my face was back but it wasn't?"

"That there was something else."

"Something else?"

"More you wanted to say. I know I don't talk much, Anna, but that doesn't stop me seeing. Is there more you wanted to say?"

Of course there was more to say, but if this were an incongruous place to talk about sex to a woman Anna had barely talked to with any real import in all her thirty-eight years, it was definitely not the place to talk about assisted suicide, that would have to wait. But she realised that however profound was the discovery and impact of sex, the knowledge of what was going to be said about Dad weighed even more heavily and showed on her face that was back but then it wasn't.

The place was filling now, and Gary Lineker and pundits were talking up England's chances v Sweden and asking would the trophy, the actual trophy that was standing proudly but Anna thought unfortunately resembling an oversized testicle in the studio beside them, be coming home? Their booming voices were piped around Cocoa Yard and mixed with the expectant buzz of the growing crowd; men and women and children, many in England shirts and some dressed like Gareth Southgate with waistcoats and masks to boot, and to a man spilling plastic drinks in hand.

"Mary," Hen said above the din, "I think Harry wants the toilet."

"Do you sweetheart?" said her mum, "Come on."

As Mary rose and took Harry's hand, Anna saw that it was too late, a dark river there for all to see if they could or if they weren't too engrossed in the theatre of dreams that were real. And with sadness she watched her mum, the little woman who she loved but had rarely talked to with any meaning until now, guide her father towards the pub where she'd clean him up in the ladies, explaining to anyone entering what was happening and it wouldn't be an issue because her dad was no threat.

"Bastard of a thing," said Daz to Anna, and again nobody disagreed.

The match was starting by the time they returned, and Anna hated those who showed mild annoyance as her mum parted the crowds to get her dad back to his seat. And then she smiled gratefully as Hen, Daz, Gord and Jigger stood to usher him in, to where they'd now join the theatre, her dad too, and they'd make a fuss of him, involve him in all the cheers and fervent analysis.

"Is Dad OK?" Anna asked her mum.

"I managed to clean him up," she said, "I brought clean pants."

"Oh, Mum, you're so good, you think of everything."

"It's hard," she said, "but I love him. And wouldn't be without him. Now he wanted us to watch the football with him so let's watch the football."

And so Anna did watch the football, with half an eye on her dad and glad he was or appeared to be finding so much enjoyment in it, with his friends and with her mum and her, the friends and the woman and the daughter he loved. "And wouldn't be without him." The words seemed loaded, pointed, so Anna knew it would be doubly-hard now to broach *that* subject. Yes that would have to wait, go unsaid that day, if even said at all.

After the football, which England won and everybody said and dared to believe they'd go all the way, Anna went to her parents' house and took her dad to bed. He was in the spare room now and this had become the norm; once he would tuck her up with a story at night, now it was her turn to do the same for him. Whereas the topic of conversation was now random, desultory or vague, it was once so clear...

Like the time they talked about Tony, to whom Dad had never taken, always just about tolerated. He'd certainly never wanted her to marry him. "I don't forget," he'd say, and list Tony's crimes against his beloved daughter; going for days on end without speaking over some minor disagreement or something she'd put in the wrong place or even over nothing tangible at all – one time he even let her cook dinner before leaving the house and returning with a takeaway curry and eating it there in front of her while the dinner she'd cooked went cold; telling her he had a surprise and she must wait with her eyes closed in the bedroom while he went downstairs to get it, and she waited for at least half an hour before realising there was no surprise at all – his 'little joke'; and worst of all the affair, which Dad had stumbled on and broke his heart over whether to tell Anna. "I hated myself more than I hated him," he'd said, "for not having the guts to tell you lest you thought I was stirring trouble, fabricating stories to make you leave that man."

Anna hated herself too, for not listening to her dad all those years ago. For not accepting his offer of money to set herself up in a flat, relying instead on Tony the higher earner and first signature on the mortgage for a house they lived in before they got married. And for not knowing the reason she didn't want kids was not this town she now hated and wouldn't want kids to grow up in, but because she didn't want them to grow up with a father like Tony. It always sounded so harsh, cruel even, when she thought of it like that, but it was true, she'd no doubt now. And about two months ago she finally owned up to it, told her dad so, and he'd seemed to understand, and hugged her and called her a crackpot and they'd laughed. And then to cheer her up he'd told her the story from when she was a kid, about a chocolate bus driver and his chocolate bus, driving his sweetheart to Cocoa Yard, Rum 'n' Raisin Road, Twix, Bounty Durham. It always made her laugh and hearing it again, now, this night, as an adult, it made her cry like a baby too.

"Did you enjoy the football, Dad?" she asked when the chocolate bus story was parked.

"Yes, thank you," he said.

"And was it nice to see your old friends again?"

"Hen," he said, "Off the buses."

"Are you all right now, Dad?"

"Tired. My bloody back."

"Mum'll be up in a minute, she'll give you your tablet." And with that he rested his eyes and she gave him a kiss night-ynight on the forehead.

"Night-ynight," he said, and when she reached the door he added, "I don't forget."

The night was still warm when she closed the door behind her and blinked away brandy-coloured tears in the streetlights. When he was like that, he was dad again. When he was telling his story about the chocolate bus driver and chocolate bus and chocolate passengers and his sweetheart, he was dad again. "I wouldn't be without him," her mother had said, and times like this when he was her husband again she'd every right to say so. What right had she, Anna, to argue otherwise? What right had Dad to say he wanted to say goodbye? It was such a cocktail of emotions as powerful as pentobarbital. And above all else at this precise moment, as Anna headed home with those tears starring her eyes, how could she say goodbye to the father she loved? What would her life be then? But she knew that this time when he said he didn't forget, he meant what they'd discussed about him wanting to die, and the signed letter he'd written to that effect, which she'd put in her bag unsealed and was yet to show her mum. Nothing vague about that at all.

The town that was dead with half-dead pigeons, that had been woken by a football match, was now falling quiet again, the drunken euphoria had worn it out and brought on sleep. Anna was worn out too, looking forward to her bed.

"Hey!" she heard a voice say, and she turned to see it was the man she took to her bed the other night, the man with whom she took control, the man who hadn't moved on when he said he would, and the man who, though she couldn't know it yet, would change everything.

"I changed my mind," he said, as they sat in the living room of her two-up two-down after she'd made coffee and asked him to excuse the mess.

"I'm glad," she said.

"And to be honest I was disappointed you weren't at the Barrel to watch the football."

"Dad wanted to go somewhere else, where there were more screens."

"I see."

"They did well."

"They did. And I stand to win a fortune if they reach the final."

"You and your betting," she said, and they smiled.

There was never any doubt in Anna's mind that when he called her in the street and caught up with her, that he would come back to her house again, and that they'd sleep together. And once again she had no delusions of this being the start of something, such was his nomadic lifestyle. But once again she was prepared to take this for what it was, enjoy the way he made love to her, the way she saw colours, the way she'd never been made love to before. Yet, their pillow-talk afterwards was somehow and somewhat different, hinting at more beyond another one-night-stand.

"I stayed because I like you," he said.

"I like you too."

"You don't suppose…" and then he tailed off.

"What? Tell me what I don't suppose."

"We could fall in love?"

The words were surprising, whispered tentatively yet meaningful, ponderous yet sincere.

"I hope so," she said.

Next day, Anna phoned in to work again and this time requested a couple of days holiday, which were owing and duly granted. They had a simple breakfast of tea and toast, then walked, hand-in-hand and as promised to his campervan on the other side of town near the retail park. It was a Renault Trafic, thirty years old he said, but solid enough. She was impressed with its facilities; toilet, sink, a little fridge with tiny freezer compartment, four-ring hob and grill.

"I have to keep it charged up," he said, "or nothing works."

"But how?" she asked.

"If I park up at a site, it has the hook-up," he said, "I charge it overnight and hey presto, I've got power for at least a week."

"It's amazing," she said.

"It's just my home that's all," he said.

"A home on wheels."

"I do like the life," he said, "the taking myself wherever I want to go. Not so good in winter of course."

"Of course. But where do you sleep?"

"I'll show you."

With some deft mechanical movements he swung the passenger seat around and slid out the rear seat so it made a bed, then reached into the storage space above the driver's seat to pull out his sleeping bag and pillow, which he explained were heavy tog, mountaineers' kit.

"What great fun!" she said, "But do you ever get scared?"

"It's a way of life that's become accepted," he said, "there are thousands of people doing it, some of them made homeless, some of them just opting out. I get the odd car horn from people who think I'm in a layby having sex. Otherwise I'm left alone."

"I wonder," she said, suddenly struck by a thought, "could we sleep in here tonight? I can't believe I said that!"

"Sure," he said, "It's two-berth. But it needs hooking up or I won't be able to make you a cuppa in the morning."

"You could park it in my drive!" she said, fired up now, "You could hook up to my mains couldn't you?"

"I could," he said, a little doubtful.

"Come on!" she said, "It'll be great fun!"

"If you're sure."

While it was a huge surprise for Anna to be suggesting such things that she'd never for a minute imagined, it was tremendously exciting. Here she was, the woman with a little house and a little job, who hadn't done anything extraordinary ever, begging this man who'd walked into her life to spend a night in his campervan! She wondered what her so-called friends at work would make of this, and what the neighbours would think, and what, more pertinently, her mother and father would make of it too?

And so it happened that Walker's Renault Trafic was parked beside her house, plugged in to her mains, and for the days and weeks that followed they'd be alternating between the van and the house to spend their nights together. It didn't matter that the neighbours twitched their curtains and probably thought it a little odd, it didn't make any difference that her friends at work privately scoffed at the idea when she told them she had a new bloke who lived in a campervan and she lived in it with him part-time, what mattered was that she was having life breathed into her, that she was falling in love with this exotic, leather-skinned man… But what mattered most of all was that she was happy and her parents were happy *for* her.

"I knew you were Bohemian when we met you that day," said Mary, the night Anna first took Walker to her parents'.

"Bohemian?" said Walker, glancing at Anna, who herself was surprised to hear her mum use such a word.

"A little different. The way you were sitting there alone with your paper, in your hat and your shorts and your tanned legs showing. I knew you were one who liked to get out in the sun, to travel."

"He's been to some wonderful places," said Anna, amused at her mum's cackhanded description.

"I was on the buses," said Harry, "Thirty years over."

"I know," said Walker, "Anna said you were very popular, very dedicated."

"Dedicated," he said, and Mary beamed with happiness at her husband's rare display of lucidity. It was as if this handsome stranger had brought with him some elixir, some rejuvenating placebo perhaps, or at the very least the energy to incentivise the man to converse somewhere near the level on which he used to.

"Thank you very much for coming to see us," Mary said, when Walker and Anna were preparing to leave.

"It's been a pleasure to meet you again," he said.

"But I can't call you Walker of course."

"Of course."

"I want to call you Terry," she said.

"Terry," said Harry.

"Goodnight, Harry," said Walker.

"You live on a bus?" he asked.

"A campervan," said Terry, "though I suppose it's kind of a bus in a way."

"A mini-bus," said Anna.

"Day Return to Cocoa Yard please?" said Harry, with a coded smile to Anna.

That night it was the turn of the campervan to provide shelter for Anna and Walker, and as they bedded down together in their sleeping bags and kissed goodnight, Anna said how proud she was of Walker for being so friendly towards her parents, and she couldn't remember how long it was since she'd been so proud. Her husband Tony had never been made so welcome into her parents' house, her dad had never liked him, but clearly her dad liked Walker, in other words it was a seal of approval. Pleased, Walker said it was genuinely a nice evening.

"But what does he mean by 'Day Return to Cocoa Yard'?" he asked.

"It was that story he used to tell me when I was a child," she said, "a story about a chocolate bus with a chocolate driver who drove his sweetheart to Cocoa Yard, Rum 'n' Raisin Road, Twix, Bounty Durham."

"That's wonderful," he said with a chuckle, adding "Though other brands are of course available." And then he kicked himself for demeaning their story with a hackneyed joke.

"When you went to the loo," she said, "Dad said how much he liked you and Mum agreed. She said you're good for me."

"I want to be."

"Hey I've got an idea," she said, "Dad goes to the day centre tomorrow to give mum her respite. How about we run him there in this?"

"We could," he said, "if it's OK with your mum?"

"I'm sure," she said, "and anyway I quite fancy another ride in her."

"As the actress said to the chocolate bus driver," he said, and this time they both laughed.

And then they slept, for Anna the blissful sleep that was only possible because she'd had such a lovely evening, when her dad was lucid, the strong man he used to be, more like the dad she used to have, and whose letter of intent about assisted suicide lay for now unsealed and forgotten in her bag. And, for now, she hadn't needed to explain to Walker that the story he invented for her had been recently adapted to mean that Cocoa Yard was the place the chocolate bus driver would go when his days were over.

They were up early next morning and prepped expeditiously for the day ahead, when they'd drive to Anna's parents and run them to the day centre. She'd phoned ahead to tell her mother the plan and she'd agreed, saying it would make a pleasant change for Dad, take him out of himself.

"Oh, Terry, what a lovely old van," she said when they arrived.

"Thanks," said Walker, mock-offended at the word old.

"Diesel," said Harry, as Anna helped him into the passenger seat.

"Yep," said Walker, "no power-steering but she goes like a dream."

Once Anna had belted Harry in, and she and Mary were safely in the two rear passenger seats, Walker revved the engine and the van headed throbbingly through the town of Marlin and more smoothly now the engine was warm into the busier Harrogate Road. From the rear, Mary gave Anna a nudge and nodded towards Harry, who they could see was smiling, gazing out at the moving buildings and giving a wave to schoolchildren.

"He's back," said Mary.

"What do you think, Dad?" asked Anna.

"The wheels on the bus go round and round," he sang, and as Mary joined in, the tears streaming down her cheeks, she leant towards Anna and said,

"I want you to show me the letter."

*

"What letter?" asked Walker when they'd dropped Mary back at home.

"The one Dad wrote," said Anna and now told Walker for the first time what she'd been harbouring ever since the night her dad gave it to her, and said it was time, it was something he wanted to do and had decided while he was still *compos mentis* enough, or "still had enough marbles" as he termed it. That he wanted to say goodbye to the two women he loved, and have them remember him while he still had some strength of body and soundness of mind.

"And did you show her?" asked Walker, shocked and moved by the concern now furrowed on beautiful Anna's face.

"Not yet. I said I'd take it to her this afternoon."

"Would you like me to come with you?"

"No. Thank you. I think this should just be me and Mum."

"I fully respect that," he said.

As Anna left the little two-up two-down she called home, with a campervan parked incongruously in the drive, probably to some of the neighbours' amusement or irritation as they twitched their curtains, and headed up the street towards the part of the town where her parents lived, there was an air of peace and tranquillity. The weather now was turning and the heat and fervour of World Cup England with its bunting and jingoism had now been slept on and left behind, for the town to keep on resting the way it had for the past ten years. Most of the shops were shuttered or boarded up, while the ones that remained seemed tired, moribund, selling out to the tide of out-of-town retail parks. "Closing down sale," said ABC Electricals, "Everything must go." Anna reflected on that, and thought it was poignant, symbolic, that everything must go, that the town had had an injection of energy, however brief, and now was fading, like her dad had had an injection of energy, itself only brief, because he wanted to go to sleep. The doctors had given indications. Yes, it could go on for weeks, months, even years the way Alzheimer's is, one couldn't tell, but it was certainly not something that he'd return from. In other words, it was terminal. She also knew that if, and it was a very big if, her mother read the letter and agreed to her father's wishes, they had to go through hoops to make it happen, face some very harsh moral questions and possibly castigations should word get out. *If word got out?* she thought to herself, *Got out to whom?* Mum had no other relatives and very few friends and neither did she. Of course there were her father's old friends Gordon, Hen and co., but what could they say if they knew? What could they do? Nothing, because this was a matter, a family matter not even involving Walker, but between herself, her mum and the man who wanted to die with dignity.

With shaking hands, Mary took the envelope that Anna offered, that had been kept unsealed and pristine in her handbag upstairs, deftly opened it, and read:

"My dearest Mary

I hope that by the time you read this we will have discussed it, but I write it for two reasons, to make formal my wishes and to convey the things that one can't do in discussion which can become clouded by emotion or argument.

That's not to say that I don't expect the contents of the discussion to be taken lightly by you, because they are or can be profoundly upsetting.

I have loved you all these years my darling, you've been there by my side through thick and thin, you've been there to amuse me when I've been down and give me attention when I've craved it. All these years you've been unfailing in your love for me and your support when I've been ill.

We've known for some time that I have Alzheimer's, of course we didn't recognise it at first, when I started to get forgetful, clumsy, and it didn't fully register when Doctor Jenkin-Jones first diagnosed me. Even when I retired from the buses and then began to make mistakes when driving our car, we didn't, or couldn't, face what was happening. But now of course we have, yet you've still been there with me throughout as things have got worse and worse. And we've even laughed about it, like the time I took my eyebrows off on the cooker!

I know I can linger on like this for several months or even years, and that there's no way back, but I want you to know that the decision I have made, and have discussed with our beautiful daughter, has been made at a time when I can describe the way I feel, convey my final wishes. It might be hard for you to know that I discussed it with Anna before I discussed it with you, but please believe me when I say that I did so only to spare your feelings. I suppose I wanted to use Anna as a sounding-board, though I hope she won't see it like that. I hope she'll see it, like you will see it, as me just wanting to build up to telling you. You know that Anna and I have always been so close, that from the time when she was a beautiful little girl and I told her stories at bedtime, teaching her to ride a bike called Lavender, to when she finally left the family home, she's been the apple of my eye, someone I've always cherished and someone I've always seen as a gift from you to me. I was as you know heart-broken when she got married to that man, and sometimes I'm sorry I felt like that, that I couldn't take to the man or even call him by his name. And I sometimes feel guilty for taking pleasure in their break-up and subsequent divorce. I know this caused her much pain, but I truly hope that one day, before I die, she'll meet someone she can love and who can love her back the way she deserves.

And so my darling, I come to the point where I have to write the words I want to write. That at such a time when Anna meets someone, and if she is happy, and if I still have my marbles, I wish to die a dignified death, I wish to say goodbye to this world and this awful 'thing' before it gets too bad, it gets to the point when I become aggressive like my mother did, and I don't know you, when I'm in a home and you come and see me and I'm sitting vacant in a chair, staring through a window and smelling of pee and accusing people of stealing my money.

I don't want that my darling. I want to go when I know you, when I remember the happiness we had together, when we can still talk and laugh about things, when I can still be in the driving seat of the bus.

I repeat that I know this will be upsetting for you to read, and the weeks leading up to the event should you accept my wish will be heart-rendingly difficult, but I beg that you can come to understand and appreciate my words and finally come to terms with them. It would be one final gift and demonstration of your love for me, to allow me to get off the bus and go in peace and dignity and pride.

I love you my darling, I always have and I always will, and I hope you will see the sense of my going when I know you, and you can remember me as the strong, hardworking, loving man I always tried to be.

Yours ever,
Harry x
The Chocolate Bus Driver,
Cocoa Yard.
Rum 'n' Raisin Road
Twix
Bounty Durham"

Anna had sat silently watching her mother read the words with trembling hands and heaving chest. And when she finished she went and sat beside her on the settee and held her hand.

"I know, Mum," she said, "I know."

*

In the weeks that followed the day that Anna and her mother discussed the contents of her father's letter, several momentous things happened. She told Walker that night about her father's wishes, how in private moments he'd told her what he wanted and that he was not made of chocolate, he was strong enough to make the decision, and how it turned out her mother had known all along – her father had broached the subject one night and she was upset and angry. They'd fallen out about it in the way they'd never fallen out about anything before. She told Anna that seeing Harry that day in Terry's van, singing The Wheels on the Bus, she really did think he was back, but in her heart of hearts she knew it was just a short journey and there was sense in his argument and there could come a time to take it seriously. That also in her heart of hearts she'd choose to lose him while he was lucid enough to know her, while he was strong enough to be like the man she'd loved all those years, and that's how she'd prefer, in her heart

165

of hearts, to remember him. She could no longer be two people, one who couldn't bear to see him suffer and the other who couldn't bear to lose him.

Walker too was shocked at first to hear all this. It wasn't that he was particularly against the idea on moral grounds, more that he was worried about the toll it would take on Anna and her mother. But then he began to see the sense in a person wanting to die in dignity, when he was able to recognise his beloved wife and beautiful daughter. Walker had fallen deeply in love with Anna, and over time they'd spent increasing amounts in her house as opposed to his van. The sale of it was mooted but ruled out lest they'd want to use it to go for days or weekends out, to the countryside or the coast. But given his increasing number of nights indoors, where he'd share the housework and the cooking, it was decided he'd have his own key. And with that, in his view, came the responsibility to pay his way, and to that end he'd quit gambling and taken a job in the B&Q warehouse on the retail park outside the town. He was back on the grid and settled into it with relish and with ease, and made sure the bills and the mortgage were paid equally. Life for him now had some meaning, he said, and there was some hope that wasn't written on a betting slip. And then, quite out of the blue, he proposed to her, and she said yes, and when they told her parents they were over the moon. For Anna, the love she felt for Walker had deepened too, and the more she loved him the more she forgot Tony, the man still wearing the chinos she bought for him from George, and his cruelty, and the fact she didn't want children to grow up with a father like him. Not that she'd ever want children now, far too late for that. She'd come to terms with that, and come to realise she'd at last found a man she wanted to live with for the rest of her life, and so when he proposed she said yes without hesitation. And now, after years and years of irritation and self-consciousness, her eczema had virtually vanished. The town of Marlin was, on the back of a strong summer of commerce, making something of a comeback. The ABC Electrical store enjoyed a renaissance, a brand-new spark, as did other units along the high street. Even the pound bakery had been given a lick of paint. A ring road was being built, encircling new housing estates that were going up with impressive rapidness, and young families were moving in to them. The pubs were doing well, The Barrel especially with its nightly functions: karaoke, quizzes with cash prizes, live bands. England did not win the World Cup, they fell at the second to last, yet somehow this was still a victory of open-topped bus proportions. Ange the barmaid was still part of the fixtures and fittings and planning a second visit to Andalucia because she loved it the first time, but a new tenant had taken over with fresh ideas, innovative measures that mixed the traditional with the modern so the likes of Gordon and co. could enjoy leaning on the newly-varnished bar as much as the younger blood that would come to its music. The Council had commissioned a cull of the pigeons that shat everywhere, so it was a far more wholesome and, Anna realised, attractive little market town atmosphere. For Anna's parents of course, the weeks that followed were not easy, but slowly and gradually things were put in place, no political, medical or moral stone unturned. It wasn't easy for Anna to contemplate the moment when it would happen. Of course, she'd done her research on the internet, spoken to doctors, spoken even to her boss at work when she explained she'd need to take a two-week break because she was going to Switzerland. She knew that come the day it would be heart-breakingly painful, that her father would go through the legal process, be asked more than once if he was sure. She knew that she'd be on one side of him and mum would be on the other, holding his hand while the administrator asked, "Are you sure that you want to drink this medicament with which you will sleep and die?"

And her father would say, "Yes I'm sure." She knew that Walker would be waiting outside to allow the family its final moments' privacy and dignity, but be there for them when they came out. All this she knew, and knew it would be hard of course, and she'd have to make sure her mother was looked after on the journey home and beyond, and that could bring them closer together than they'd ever been before. But, in *her* heart of hearts she knew that all of this, that life itself, would be made a little easier because with Walker she had someone to love and who could give her the love that her father always said she deserved.

*

"Mystery Came to Dinner"

From the novel "Here am I Sitting in a Tin Can"

Summer 2017.

It's days like this I like the best. When the sun is shining, the North Yorkshire scenery is stunning, and I'm tootling along in a tin can, singing songs I used to know, laughing at jokes I used to tell, smoking spliffs and not giving a flying fuck that I'm holding up the traffic behind me because this thing can only do a maximum of fifty. Days like this when I feel beyond doubt that I made the right decision to live off-grid, put my things in storage, claim the deposit back from the greedy bastard company who managed my rented apartment, waved goodbye to the wankers and the contortionists I once had the misfortune of working with, and took to the road. Days like this in isolation, blissfully happy and thinking one day everybody will live like this. One day in the not too distant, when either it's everybody's choice or some horrible chemical warfare or wilful destruction of the planet that will deem it necessary, vital or compulsory. Days like this when I say, "I want to be alone. So who would like to join me?"

Trawling through recent memory and tarmac covered, I consider the beehived barmaid of Bridlington who reminded me of Bet Lynch, the lady in Annan who bemoaned the loss of the post office and the town council's lack of forward-planning, Ann the poor bereft damsel in Scarborough perhaps…? The list is endless yet notional, my options far-reaching yet limited.

Staithes is the destination of choice today, but first I need provisions. I'm in the mood, I'm planning a romantic dinner for one, a bottle of wine or two to see me through another night of stealth, listening to waves nearby and gazing at stars a million miles away. Just as I'm docked in the deep end of Asda carpark away from the lazy bastards who need to be almost in the entrance to save their fattened legs, and I'm locking up the tin can, I hear a voice:

"Excuse me," it says, "You dropped your wallet." She is petite, blonde and pretty, dressed casually in black.

"Thanks."

"You're welcome," she says, and grins a toothy grin and proceeds to load her shop into her little Kia. Under normal circumstances, exchanges such as this would end right there, but today my needs are different.

"I'm on my way to Staithes," I say.

"It's nice there," she says.

"So I believe."

"And are you staying over in that?"

"I am," I confirm, not at all offended by the slight disparagement in her tone, "Hotel Tin Can."

"I didn't mean to sound rude," she says.

"Not at all. It's not much but it's my home."

"You live in it?" she says, "How wonderful!"

Chicken is what I decide on, so I'm traipsing the aisles choosing the veg to accompany and a nice bottle of wine. I am only a connoisseur of under-a-fiver plonk, but find myself for once looking upwards. Chateauneuf du Pape is what I see and like the sound of, so I take a couple down and read the label. "Chateuneuf du Pape," I say aloud, relishing the way it rolls off the tongue, "Or seventeen quid a pop."

Four hours later I've reached my destination, a rural spot up the steep hill from the harbour, and the four rings on my cooker are fired up with bubbling pans. There is no greater pleasure than cooking a meal for a woman. Except when she eats it, and manages to keep it down. But I'm uncharacteristically nervous. I've changed from combats into smartish jeans and a shirt that hasn't been ironed but will pass. I'm weighing up the odds, thinking how strange a life like this can be and how brave was my asking her to dinner. And how ridiculous it is that I'm expecting her to show. A stranger in a supermarket carpark, a traveller travelling to find a story, a man who hasn't shaved for weeks and a pretty woman having dinner in a tin can? What kind of fool could expect this to end any other way than disappointingly? Yet it's no mean feat to juggle pans on four rings burning, and no mean feast I see before me that will bless the plastic plates should the lady reappear.

She is dressed in purple now, slim-fitting and perfect with her crooked smile. Her talk is somewhere northeast and lyrical, accompanied by bangles, and her hair is tied back to show ears with dripping silver. Maybe she's nervous too, though she doesn't seem so. I pour the Chateauneuf du Pape and we chink plastic glasses as I disclaimer the culinary fare. But she puts her hand on mine and with that toothy smile she says, "It's lovely. I've never had dinner on a van before."

I'm embarrassed. I've never been comfortable with compliments, it's something I hate about myself, but I came to learn that following a compliment there comes a knife in the back. Such scars are indelible.

But she eats every last plastic-forked morsel as between each morsel she tells me things about her life. And between each morsel I watch and listen. Her face is fascinating too. She offers to wash the plastic but I gratefully decline.

"I'll do it in the morning," I venture, hoping the "I" would be "we", and suggest instead a walk. There are beaches to comb.

We comb for miles on end, chatting, laughing, and in Robin Hood's Bay I take her hand in order to help negotiate some slippery rocks. I don't think she really needs help, but the ruse has worked because we remain hand-in-hand for the rest of the walk, talking constantly, laughing often. She finds a stripy stone and picks it up to clean. I ask if that's significant or lucky and she says no, she just likes stripy stones, she collects them. And then we finally reach a quiet cove to rest.

It was from my mother I learned that in the films they cut to rolling waves. And afterwards I tell her so and sadly she is dead.

"You must miss her," she says, straightening her skirt.

"I do," I say.

And then we journey back, hand-in-hand, this time silence speaking volumes against the gentler tidal sibilance of sea and air.

Hotel Tin Can is waiting when we get there, and I hope she'll share my room for the night, open the second bottle. But she can't, she says, she has to get back. Though I want to, I don't ask why or to whom. "Thank you for a lovely time," she says, yet we talk for ages more. I tell her about my life as a nomad, days in isolation, we sing, I strum my ukulele, we enjoy being silly, till finally we kiss goodbye, and off into the night she disappears.

Later, when my plastic plate is washed, I add the stripy stone to my collection, finish the wine, gaze at the stars a million miles away and smoke another joint.

*

"Orange Dog—the Diary of Malcolm B"

One day that is unbearable.

You will have noticed I've been quiet of late. It's because I am suicidal. Believe me I am. I've had enough, I've had all I can take. Each moment from now is a moment closer to the first car. This horrible monster is back with cruel vengeance. I look in the mirror and hear a voice, I see the face of someone else. For some the colour of this thing is dark; for me it is orange meaning everything I see has this orange haze like looking through a Quality Street wrapper or a camera whose lens has that Lucozade-coloured filter. It caves in my head— it aches like mad! The more I try to push the colour aside, the harder it is to banish the thoughts that come with it. Bad thoughts—unbeatable. Bad words. Loneliness when all my loved ones are travelling from far and wide to see me fill my room with smoke, doing all they can; when friends are phoning, texting, doing all they can too. Still loneliness—despair—still despair and still all the other crap that comes with life for the millions of people like me and the millions not like me too. Bereavement—yes! I've had my share—regrets! I've had a few—not too few to mention, cracked relationships— tick, unemployment—tick and thanks to the bastards, I sweated blood for poverty. Inevitably homelessness! Oh yes, but what can you do? Only try to crawl your way back from the gutter which mercifully I did. I *clawed* my way back. I found work. I found love, a nice apartment yet the monster couldn't or wouldn't leave me alone. It moved in with me un-invited, lugged its cheap and nasty chattels into my home when I wasn't looking and refused to leave me alone to get on with my life in peace… Anger—oh, definitely anger at success is past my moments turned to memory and creased photographs; Anger on behalf of those whose mental health is misunderstood by heartless, gutless employers whose only answer is to manage out the problem when others, young, untroubled by brains warm their fat posteriors on vacant chairs. Anger at the email that once did for me that was meant for the boss and mistakenly went to me and I did nothing because I chose to rise above the currency of petty tittle-tattle. Libel. Slander. Anger at the monster who warned me I was weak— too nice that magnanimity would cost me and it was right! Anger at all the people who *ever* hurt me—smug-faced bullies, mouth of the Irwell with knitting needles, big-brain assassins and those who can't look you in the eye. Anger on behalf of professionals who do understand the epidemic and do their best under pressure and with resources stretched to their limit. Anger with *myself* for being angry when all these things are spent for allowing my mind to dwell on those for whom I shouldn't waste my breath or words —those whom I should unfollow, with myself for hurting others for I have been no saint and I am only human after all; with myself for being negative about all that and everything else—hatred of all the evils in the world—hatred of myself again—hatred even of the fact that sometimes, yes sometimes, if I'm frank, I find some weird masochistic gratification from the pain; does anybody know what I mean? "Maybe it's psychosomatic or the voices in my head that make me worry too much" Bill said. Medication—I've had it all. I've touched the sun on cocktails of diazepam venlafaxine mirtazapine and come down mourning an addled and cloudy mind that only wants to say

"You Want To Die!"

But for millions like me, negativity is what life *is*—negativity is all you see, negativity—loneliness—lovelessness— waste and pointlessness coated in orange-coloured tasteless sugar. Mental Health Awareness Week! I watched programmes on my TV and applauded, welcomed the positivity that things are improving; society is working with me erasing the stigma and encouraging me to talk. I've talked—I've talked and talked yet nothing I say has any meaning just a string of words struggling to convey what's in the yoke of my mind but it's not enough. A week is not enough when a thing has a week-long run to own a stage; the curtain then will fall—the audience will file out of the theatre having had an experience they may talk about it—they may even resolve to act but soon another experience grabs the spotlight of their lives and they forget as is their way and as is their right of course, because

"Nobody Really Knows!"

And I'm scared! I'm scared, the more the dog is barked, the more compassion fatigue could fester—the more impostors might be prone to "impost". See the problem is this thing—this orange dog can go invisible, sneak around the corridors, skulk in the stationery cupboard or go unnoticed at the watercooler. So could it be that when one feels a little down or fancies swinging the lead, he may say I have depression? It's the modern way, the dawn of the badge—the plastic bagful of allergies off the peg at "Accessorise"—the age of the hypochondriac who has flu when it's a common cold, lumbago when it's an achy back from sitting for too long in a computer screen because the pacey wheels of industry will leave skid marks for nobody—a migraine when it's nothing a couple of aspirin couldn't shift. I swear to dog backwards I am not a liar! I look well but I am ill—I smile at you but I am bad. I fill my glass at the watercooler and say yes it's a lovely day but I want it to be my last.

Why?

I travelled, got a day return to my past. I saw a happy child loving parents and four older brothers. The house was a happy one, not rich, not poor, just happy, with full ashtrays and bellies of laughs. I saw the beginning of the 70s, when I was seven in baggy-arsed trousers, sitting in the garden with my brothers, listening to the wireless. Cat Stevens, Matthew and son. Inside the house, there was the day we got our first colour television and how exciting was that? Then later there was a phone, two-tone green, which we all raced to answer when it rang, pushing and shoving and wedging each other into the hall doorway. There was the egg man who came every Sunday a homosexual though it wasn't talked about, the pop van that fetched cream soda, Tizer, Dandelion and Burdock, and on Thursdays there'd be the coal wagon and a blackened man with elephantiasis lugging sacks on his bare back—Dad showing me how to hold an axe and chop sticks for starting the fire.

Christmases special, looked forward to for months— crates of pale ale, cans of Double Diamond that worked wonders, Watneys Party 7s, Egg Flip that remained unopened and turned to custard till it got chucked in the bin sometime the following June. Ads on the telly for Hi Karate aftershave and K-Tel records, gnawing chocolate brazils like squirrels and leaving the dates. We played cards for pennies and laughter filled the smoky air. Dad would chew his only cigar of the year. The telly never went on until Morecambe and Wise. We got 45rpm records costing 45p; Mud, Sweet, the Glitter Band, T-rex, Quatro, Hendrix, and we all sang *Sugar Baby Love* and *I Love You Love* till the veins stuck out on our necks—all taped for posterity on a crackling reel to reel, stealing chocolate mice from Gandhi's shop.

Amid there'd be the happy little baggy-arsed kid feeling a loneliness in a room full of men, a sadness in the laughter, only noticed by his mother, the sole woman in the house most often to be found in the kitchen powerfully beating eggs and happy with it—always the sweet smell of butterfly cakes and Dream Topping. Something she called Sherry Delights. She asked him why he cried and he didn't know why because depression was not spoken of, not diagnosed, not invented, seen and not heard and anyway so easily shrugged off because it was the decade to be happy; the decade when we all were becoming richer. It was the decade to have fun on a Chopper bike. Innocence, celebrated naivety, big wallpaper, loud glam rock two drummers, brilliantly-camp party songs by singers in flares and platform shoes till punk gave it a kick in the bollocks with a Doc Marten boot come 76. And I'd be listening to the Pistols now not Stevens; not in the garden but in the bathroom, counting my pubic hairs and measuring my knob which rose gentlemanly to the thought of a girl I fancied at school—jailbait for pubescents. My brothers were already out driving Beetles and Hillman Imps and shagging girls disguising lovebites.

Some of the best days of my life. If I could, right now, here this minute, I'd gather up all the good things that happened to me then and since, all the success and all the travel that means the world, meaningful relationships, four beautiful kids, two beautiful grandkids—I'd gather everything good into a giant sack, lug it on bare-back into the 70s, have a cup of cold coffee and a piece of cake and preserve it there for ever. Yet sickeningly, nostalgia is just a lozenge and I only want to say I'll see myself out.

A day later that seemed like months.

I'll see myself out.

Some days later that seemed like purgatory.

Imagine hanging yourself. Fixing two leather belts together, strapping them around the joists of an outbuilding, noosing it around your neck. Then saying goodbye to the world you view as cruel, the person you view as hopeless. Jumping from the ladder to your death.

That's what I did. I really did, and all I got was whiplash and a twisted ankle. Because I have strength and my depression is its curse, and I have high standards, I should've been at best disappointed with the result and at worst well suicidal. I was in a very bad place. The world blood orange. No work—no money—no food—no tobacco. Debts piling, unopened reminders and threats conspiring in a closed drawer. I'd stopped writing. It wasn't writer's block—I don't believe in all that crap—plenty of stories to tell, lots to say, just couldn't be bothered to say it. I'd go for walks to clear my head, pop the dolly mixtures as instructed and talk about how I felt my life was shit. Yes, I had family, a girlfriend, friends all around me;

yes, the sun was shining in my window, yes, there was a roof over my head, there were crosswords to do, books to read, tins to eat, tea bags to drink and love to love. But none of these things, good things, were sufficient to take away the orange fug of loneliness, despair, poverty and hopelessness that was crushing my brain and paralysing my body. The feeling of wanting to be alone and hating the isolation, and the unbearably sapping boredom, whereby I'd forego a bowel movement in the morning because it'd leave me with nothing to do in the afternoon. And yes, I'd talk, enough to have a donkey limping, and feel bad because everybody has a limit. They have things going on in their lives too so why would they want to listen to you? Why would they want to waste their time with you when they could be wasting it on themselves? Why would they want to read what you write about this shit when they could be having fun? That's how it feels. So I gave an acceptance speech to myself, celebrating a sometimes successful career and exploring funny anecdotes from a forgotten world and acknowledging it was over. Fifty-five, I said, so that, it would seem, is that. But sometimes laughter turns to anger as you begin to question why? Why should it be over? You've spent thirty years helping others carve careers far better than the one you carved for yourself, so why shouldn't you wonder if someone could do you a favour in return—give you a lifeline? You shouldn't because you know life just doesn't work like that, it's every fucker for himself—contacts are as contactless as your credit card. So you finally deduce that the answer to the question, *why is it over* is *because it just is*. Accept it, stop whinging, leave the podium, shut the fuck up— get better. So that's what you do. But it's not easy. Universal Credit—universally murder, not enough to live on—not enough to eat. Whichever arsehole thought that one up should be forced to try it, see what it feels like to grovel at the food bank. Apply and get turned down for jobs you're overqualified for or not even qualified for at all. You disembowel your phone, deleting fair-weather numbers, quick-fix ephemeral relief for your system which is actually in decay. Spiralling rapidly, falling fast into the abyss, the colour of your depression creeping its way back into your mind and no matter how many loving people and all-weather friends there are around you—saying and doing all the right things—you finally stop listening and decide instead that life or what pitifully calls itself that is not worth living any more. That's where I was—in that very dark place. Fixing two leather belts together, strapping them around the joists of an outbuilding, noosing it around my neck. Moments earlier I'd written my last post. Within moments of pressing "publish", I was closing my laptop, putting out all the carefully written letters to those I love on the table, making sure I was dressed smart but casual because I wanted to die in some sort of dignity even in a bin shed—photos of my kids and my parents and my brothers in my inside jacket pocket near my heart—venturing outside for one last smoke. Puffing happily to the outside world, on the canal side, listening to birds singing, colliding tunefully with the stark discordant finality of what I was about to do. Soon, I was flicking my cigarette butt into the cut and then angry with myself for making litter, I was heading towards my destination—the bin shed of the apartments where I live, carefully chosen and with not a little irony because I was rubbish. This was no cry for help. I was tired of those! No, this was the end. I'd made sure nobody knew! I was there! I'd locked the door from the inside and left notes for the police if I'm brutally frank. I'd enjoyed the macabre subterfuge, a mental moving story with suspense and I was the handsome hero, the belts were strong leather one of which I bought over thirty years ago—one more recently for fifty pounds, a mere snip in affluent times. I'd tested their resistance clung onto them with my hands and let them take my not inconsiderable weight and let it swing all good. All going to plan, not a single stone unturned and then, saying goodbye to the world I viewed as cruel the person I viewed as hopeless pausing for just a second to ask if I was sure. Taking a breath. And jumping, wanting my neck to snap.

But that didn't happen the world did not turn black My neck it did not snap, the belt I bought more recently for fifty pounds, a mere snip in affluent times, snapped instead. As the ladders clattered to the floor and I was suspended on the cusp of death for maybe just a nano-second, I plunged to the concrete floor, gasping for breath, badly twisting my ankle and experiencing the judder of whiplash. I lay there for some moments in the putrid stench of bins, trying to take stock, scared, shaking, confused, even asking myself if I were alive or dead. Was this what death feels like? And then the pain in my ankle told me it was the former. "Fuck!" I cried. Fifty quid, a mere snip in more affluent times for a piece of shit, when the belt I got for a fiver, thirty years ago was intact—something I could still rely on. How standards these days have slipped! "Fuck!" I cried again at the injustice.

Moments later a complete idiot and failure, I was in my apartment with a strong coffee, spilling hopelessly in my shaking hands, unread notes still on the table in front of me, my foot and neck sore and throbbing—sweating with the rush of adrenaline and confusion. What to do next? What can I use? And then my phone begins to ring and it's my beloved son, who'd read what I'd written and was naturally worried... It was the first of many calls from guardian angels.

I feel I must apologise for the ominous, blunt and provocative tone of those four words I wrote. I'll see myself out. Frankly however it was deliberately dramatic—four simple words summing up the destructive emotions of anger, sarcasm, existentialism and self-loathing that fuel my depression. But as I sat waiting for Miranda, upset coffee becoming skinned, I began to question who was the guardian angel who made the belt snap—who wasn't yet ready for me to leave this world? I'm far from a religious man but perhaps there really *was* someone up there, out there, somewhere, or *something*—some entity, some force, up there, out there, somewhere, that wanted me alive, to live on. If that is indeed the case, it offers me yet another question—*why*? *Why* was she, or he, or it, helping me live on? And if it's to live on for yet more shit and misery I'd rather she or he or it hadn't bothered. Then suddenly, out of nowhere, sitting there with my left foot throbbing and my neck still stiffening, I begin to laugh. "Story of your fucking life," I say aloud with a gallows chuckle, "You couldn't even get *that* right! Next you'll be jumping from the window of your ground floor flat!" I don't denigrate or undermine the severity of the problem, because something's seriously wrong. It's horrible, it's frightening, and it's happening everywhere—it's happening right now and it's happening to me.

So I'm in the system again, waiting for phone calls from medics and shrinks, needing to be assessed, frustrated and angry that the poor bastards trying to help me are stretched to the limit. Will it be ECT or will it be changing the tablets again? It seems to go on for ever and they deserve better. As for me, well, I'll be going to the bloke who sold me the belt in far more affluent times and asking for a refund. And as for wanting to die, that's just something I must live with.

A week or so later…

In the waking hours since trying to get to the big sleep, I've been overwhelmed by many emotions including fear; that my writings in these pages will be met with compassion fatigue. But writing is all I do, it's all I *can* do, and I tell myself that if someone somewhere reads these words and it moves them or even makes them think twice, they're worth exploring, worth saying, worth the risk of tiring people out with their pessimistic gloom. So with emphasis on the positive, the sheer number of responses to my existential crisis and their heartfelt message has deeply moved me. Words of encouragement, reassurance and beauty—the likes of which I could only dream of penning and for which I can only give thanks—they are truly, truly welcome—they are missives of all-weather friendships and love that make me realise just how many people *truly* care, and remind me there is a phoenix of hope lurking somewhere amid the flames of anger, poverty, worthlessness, despair—the fires of jobless hell where the devil puts in overtime.

However, and this is an emotion I'm struggling to come to terms with or even describe; I can't help feeling guilt. For instance, if I were totally alone in my depression, if I had not a single loved-one, family member or friend, then the dramatic starkness of what I did in trying to take my own life would affect (apart of course from the person/people who found me) only one person…me. But a person like me who is lucky enough to be surrounded by many carers and genuine well-wishers, knows his death would cause wider-spread grief and devastation. So when these guardian angels come from corners of this world to see him, he feels bad about their being inconvenienced. It isn't actually the case, they call or come out of love, their crusade is not inconvenience, but it's just how he *feels*, because his illness is like that—it wants to eat into his mind and make him think only darkly, negatively, destructively.

So these past few days have fetched a bowl of emotions whisked as hard as my mother whisked eggs, most of them positive, a few of them negative and paranoid. Among the many calls, there have been a couple of withheld numbers, which I've answered and heard nothing. There's definitely someone at the other end but after a few seconds of this nothingness, the caller has hung up. I confess this makes me wonder, and while paranoia tries to seep its way into my confused mind, it convinces me this was one of the knitters at the guillotine. I manage to keep it at bay, preferring to think the caller either just wanted to hear my voice to know I was OK or couldn't bring himself to speak. But sometimes tough love and harsh words are entirely appropriate, like when my son arrived and said in his wonderfully demotic way, "Give me a hug you fucking nut-job." I laughed and talked at length, trying with heroic effort to convey how all this feels. Long speeches that've made my mouth and lips sandbanks, that've made my eyes rivers, that have even made me laugh with that same gallows humour that carried me through the day I fixed my leather belts together and hung myself. Long speeches followed by silence; not the silence of the uncaring, the silence of ones who don't really know what to say. Yet they need say nothing either, because I don't expect anything. I *can't* expect anything because they've already *given* everything. And everything they've given has been wonderful, encouraging, supportive and reason to fucking live!

So what can you do? Write. *Keep* writing. Keep writing about *this*—fuck the disclaimers. Because I should no longer care about compassion fatigue and no longer feel self-conscious of these words becoming repetitive, portentous of gloom, foretelling of death. I should continue to record the wanderings of my mind and attempt to do so with truth and a condiment of levity for those who need it, and hope it'll do me and them some good. If my words can do *just one person* some good, if they can make him sit up and take notice, or if they could resonate with he who faces a similar struggle and make him see that things are not as dark as they seem, then I'm minded to say I am a happy man.

Malcolm B

*

"Baiser Au Pays Des Mille Collines"

Clutching a small paper bag of croissants, Perpetue left the patisserie in Kigali and headed to get a bus to Remera, where her brother and sisters would soon be home from school. She was tall, elegant, putting on a colourful blouse and tie-dyed jeans, with the kind of smile that only a Rwandese woman could have whereby it gleamed white below cheekbones like large conkers. She spoke Kinyarwandan, French and a tiny bit of English and said hello to one of her neighbours before moving on, deciding she'd buy some eggs and flour before catching the bus. She would be home to greet her siblings, feed their bellies then leave them with a neighbour while she went to do her work. This was a routine day for Perpetue and she was happy enough in it, but she didn't and couldn't know that it was the day that something far from routine would happen. It would be the day she'd begin to find some understanding, some reconciliation and ultimately some closure on what happened to her parents in the Genocide.

*

Elsewhere, Marcus was leaving his meeting at the Ministry of Internal Affairs and planning a quiet evening alone. He called at a small market for two bottles of Primus beer and some Embassy cigarettes before heading for the Hilltop Hotel. After a delicious steak, *bien cuit*, he took his coffee onto the verandah and sat to smoke and unwind while gazing over the luscious green hills of Kigali. This was the part of the day he'd come to like the most, time out from commerce and the politics of chaos to ease into the whistling cicadoidean nightfall and to think of those he loved back home. Those he hadn't seen for two and a half months. Sometimes he was able to phone them but sometimes the hotel's lines were dead, and on those occasions, such as tonight, it was enough to think of what his kids would be doing right now, playing in the garden perhaps, the older ones doing their homework, and the wife he loved more than anything cooking dinner and calling them all to wash their hands and sit.

"*Excusez-moi, monsieur, avez-vous fini?*"

"*Je suis desole,*" he said, "*je revais.*"

"*C'est un belle soiree, Monsieur.*"

"*Oui. Un autre s'il vous plait,*" he said.

A few moments later, the waitress returned with another cup and placed it before him.

"*Prendre plaisir,*" she said, and it was only then that he looked at her and saw that fabulous smile.

"*Merci. Quel est votre nom?*" he asked before she'd had time to leave his table.

"*Perpetue,*" she said, smiling again and in that moment he knew he wanted to know her.

He next saw her in the street in Remera, quite by chance, where he bought her a soda and over which he told her about his job with a UK coffee company, and she told him about her siblings whom she looked after because their parents were dead. Sensing her sadness, he gently asked how they died and was it in the war, and she reluctantly and softly told him yes. Remembering he'd been warned by the British Embassy not to ask such painful questions, he said he was sorry. But she told him it was OK, and explained her mother and father and uncle were lured to the Nyamata Church on the outskirts of Kigali, believing they'd find refuge, only to be slain by the machete-wielding Hutu Interahamwe Militia. She saw this happen, and managed to escape. In hiding back in Kigali, Perpetue was left to look after her younger siblings and with the help of a kindly neighbour she made the long exodus to Uganda.

After the war, she embarked on the 100-day trek back to her roots, her sisters tagging along while she carried her little brother and everything else she owned…a can for water and the clothes they stood up in. Taken in once again by neighbours, she began to eke out a living by selling cobs of corn at the roadside so she could house and feed her family and buy herself an education. Now, her siblings are six, eight and nine and she wanted to do everything possible to make sure their future might be better than hers.

Over the coming weeks, Perpetue and Marcus became friends and she would grow to call him Mutijima (kind heart). There was absolutely nothing romantic in his motives, after all he was some twenty years older than her, and her Nilotic elegance and beauty contrasted somewhat with his small, rotund stature and the face he was born with but always wished were different. No, there was nothing more in this friendship than his desire to spend time with someone pleasant, be a friend and learn more French, the language he insisted on using when they were together.

On their third meeting, she told him she had family in America and she dreamed of travelling to see them. She dreamed of seeing her siblings into college to study English and Technology. She also dreamed of saying her goodbyes to her dead parents. So one day, and only after some pleading on her part, he caved in and took her to the church where they rested…

Here, many hundreds of Tutsis and moderate Hutus were brutally murdered and their bones were now piled like a skeletal monument to the dead, and their skulls racked like hundreds of ostrich eggs, many bearing cracks where the machetes and clubs had met their target. He wanted to stand back and allow Perpetue to pick over the bones but she took his hand, begging him to go with her. Tentatively, they entered the church where layer upon layer of bones, clothes, children's books and other worldly possessions were matted between the pews, and they had no choice but to walk on them.

It felt disrespectful to trample over the dead but Perpetue said they must, to get to where she needed. At the altar, a bible lay open and a skull had been carefully placed on top. Beyond this, in what he supposed was the bombed-out chancel, were the skulls. He noticed nothing except stillness; no smell of death now, no sound except for monarch birds warbling in the eucalyptus trees. Perpetue looked over the skulls, tears in her eyes, then reached out and touched one of them.

"C'est mon pere," she said, *"Et a cote de lui c'est ma mere."*

Marcus would never know how she knew it was them, or indeed *if*, but he couldn't question. Who could? She was saying her goodbyes and that was that. Then, she asked him to touch her parents too and so he did, running his finger along the cracks where the machete had fatally fallen on the heads of two people he'd never known but would never afterwards forget.

As Perpetue then knelt to pray, he stood back to leave her in the moment, and choking his own tears he could only write something probably insignificant and empty in the bloated book of condolence – what words were there to amply embrace the horror and sorrow one felt at the sight of such murderous meaningless?

"Merci," she said, *"Merci de m'avoir permis de les voir."*

In the days and weeks that followed, Perpetue would take the bus to Bugesera and visit him in the house he decided to rent once his project had been extended, where his night-guard called Joseph stationed himself in a tree and Gysenge his day-guard tended the garden with his machete. He always made sure Perpetue had food in her belly and something to take home to her brother and sisters, bananas from the garden plantation or chocolate he'd managed to find in the local supermarket. One night he played guitar for her and sang and she told him she loved him but he said he couldn't love her back because he had a wife and children at home whom he loved. He kissed her on the cheek and tasted her tears.

He visited her too, in her little hut in Remera, and met her brother and sisters, little Jean Paul, Marie Aimee and Angelique. And one day out of the blue she said,

"Je veux voir l'homme qui a tue mes parents."

Again he was unsure, doubtful, but knew this beautiful young woman was determined and would beg him till he yielded to her wishes. So he took her to Gitarama Prison, a hell-hole where it was said that inmates stood up in their own stinking shit, while ones more privileged for whatever reason would be tasked with making furniture then be drilled for miles through the streets, dressed in pink to tell the world who they were. As they sat in the car outside the gates, peering in, he wanted to know if Perpetue was sure.

"Oui je suis sur," she replied, *"Et je suis sur qu'il est le seul."*

As she pointed to one of the prisoners in pink, again Marcus could only take her at face value. And he saw this time she didn't cry. There was sadness in her eyes but nothing fell, the rivers had dried.

"Comment vous sentez-vous?" he asked.

"Rien," she said, *"Je ne sens rien. Et maintenant je veux aller a la maison."* She'd seen all she wanted to see, she'd looked into the eyes of her parents' killer, and now wanted to go home.

Over the following weeks, where Marcus and Perpetue would regularly meet, he realised he was asking himself if he *was* falling in love with her after all, but at the same time knew this was impossible. More to that, his work in Rwanda was soon to be done and he'd be heading home to Manchester via Paris, where he'd be reunited with his own family, the wife and kids he cherished.

When that day finally came, she rode the taxi with him to the airport, where they had one last drink together.

"Thank you, Mutijima," she said, in English this time, "thank you for everything you have done for me. I will never forget you kind heart."

"Thank you too," he said, "and I'm sorry I couldn't love you the way you love me."

"I understand," she said.

"But I do have a confession."

"What do you confess?"

"That day at the hotel, I didn't really want a third coffee," he said, "I made you bring it because I wanted to know you."

"I am glad. I am happy to know you too," she said and repeated that she was grateful for everything he'd done.

But on the plane, gazing down on the green pastures and coiling snakes of rivers dried, he knew he'd done very little. Yes, he'd done his best to be a friend, to encourage dreams. But what was this compared to the super-strength of a young orphan forced to mother her baby siblings, and her determination to make a better life after Genocide had taken nearly everything?

Now, many years on, when the dog comes barking and Marcus begins to feel sorry for himself, feel useless and spent in retirement back in his home town, he will often take his coffee into the garden, smoke a cigarette, listen to singing birds and think of Perpetue. He will wonder if she lived? If she managed to get her siblings into college to study English and Technology? Did she save enough to reach America and reunite with her uncles? And somehow he thinks she probably did all those things. And why? Because she was strong, she had the strength he could only envy. She'd felt the terror of being hunted, she'd witnessed her parents' screams, she'd seen the blood splash up the church walls as they were slain, their only crime to be Tutsi, she'd lived through a horror and a sadness he could barely imagine, yet he never once saw her feel sorry for herself, throw her hands in the air and cry to God why me? Why us? She'd reconciled with what had happened and found the courage to confront it, and close it, become parent to her siblings, then just got on with life. Like the gleaming white smile she smiled, she was a light that for him will never go out. She is the reason, he will now realise above all else, and ask himself why it took so long, for taking his coffee into the garden, smoking a cigarette, listening to the birds sing, and living another day.